Follow Me Here

Beca Lewis

Perception Publishing

Contents

Dedication

M y sister Jamie loved the title when I told her what the next book would be called. I had the name before the book, and as I wrote it, I came to understand what it meant.

As the months went on, she asked me when the book was going to be done. She was eager to read it. I told her she'd get the draft in mid April 2024, so she could beta read as she had every other book I've written.

But she was not around to read it by then. I was writing the last chapter as she lay dying.

Looking back, I see how helpful it was to be writing a book about loss and how life continues. I didn't know my sister would die before she read the book. I wonder if she knew. Did she understand then what *Follow Me Here* would mean to me?

The strange thing is that she had already told everyone goodbye. She had given all her friends and loved ones mementos as she gave away everything she had. She did it all because she thought she was moving to Spain, and who knew when we would see her again?

Instead, my beloved little sister, the woman who was always there for me no matter what stupid thing I did, moved someplace else, and who knows when I will see her again. But I know that I will because she will be waiting.

A few weeks before she went into the hospital, Jamie started a paid subscription to my Substack account. I cried then, because once again she was supporting me.

She said it was because, "your words matter."

So one sleepless night, when I heard a verse from the Eagles song about having "a peaceful, easy feeling, I know you won't let me down," I knew she was telling me to keep on keeping on. Her feet were already on the ground.

So I will keep writing, not just because I love to write, but because, at least to my sister, my words mattered. And that is going to have to be enough for now.

I know that there are people who arrive here who are already angels. My sister was one of them. And everyone who ever met her knew that to be the true.

Now she is free to return to the heavens where harmony reigns, and rejoin the band of angels that look after all of us. And I am grateful that she arrived in my life when I was ten and made everything better.

My sister and I always signed off our emails and letters and even phone calls to each other this way: "You are the best sister ever."

Yes, you were, Jamie.

Mary Jamison Lewis, this book is for you.

*If nothing in this world satisfies
me, perhaps it is because I was
made for another world.*
—C. S. Lewis

One

The tree branch bounced against the window, and when that didn't work, a howling gust of wind shook the glass. I rolled over and pulled the covers over my head. I was not ready to face another day. Maybe *never* face another day.

But I knew it was useless. Like every day, it was time to get up and pretend that I wanted to go downstairs, make something to eat that I didn't want, and go through a day that I didn't want to live through.

Except today. Today was different. Today was Harry's birthday. Today I wanted to live. I didn't know about tomorrow, though. That depended on what I found out today.

I reached under the covers and pulled out today's clothes. I started the habit of laying out my clothes the night before as a girl because I didn't want to have to think about what to put on in the morning. Instead, I wanted to bounce out of bed and into the world to discover what had happened while I was asleep.

That girl was long gone. But the habit remained. And when it was cold, putting them under the covers meant they were warm when I put them on.

However, the need for clothing under the covers was almost over. Spring had begun its buildup to the day everything started blooming, and the world became a jewel box for a moment in time.

But that moment was still just a promise. A few buds on the trees and some early daffodils braved the chilly wind. Outside the window, I glimpsed dark clouds filled with rain that would probably be sleet. So as much as I might wish that jeweled day to be today to help me through what was to come, it wouldn't be.

It was not as easy to get dressed under the covers as it used to be, but finally I was ready. At least I was dressed. I was certainly not ready.

Well, who would be? I muttered under my breath in the bathroom as I brushed my now gray hair and stared at the woman in the mirror.

The face that stared back at me was not one I recognized. Until I looked into a mirror, I thought of myself as still looking like I did in my late thirties, full of bright hope for the future.

As I stared at myself, I knew that woman was in there somewhere, but time had altered my features, so it always felt like I was wearing someone else's face. I caught hints of my mother in the lines on that face, and that pleased me a little. Not enough to be happy with the stranger in the mirror, though.

Behind me something flickered, and I saw Harry smiling at me, and even though I knew he wasn't really there, I smiled back. So now I was staring at a strange woman smiling at herself in the mirror.

"Stop it," I said out loud. Was it to me, or to Harry, who had left me one time too many? Probably both.

As I headed downstairs, I held onto the railing so I wouldn't slip and fall and break my neck. I pushed away the idea that maybe that would be a good thing. Only because I couldn't count on dying. What if I ended up paralyzed in a chair being pushed by someone who I didn't know and probably wouldn't like?

"Dark thoughts, Mabel," I heard Harry say.

"Shut up," I wanted to say back to him, but what good would that do? He wasn't here, anyway. Hence the dark thoughts.

By the time I finished swearing at nobody in particular and everything in general, I reached the bottom of the stairs. I had learned to swear long ago in high school, and the urge to swear and the pleasure of certain words that shouldn't be said rolled around on my tongue, making me smile again.

A small rebellion, perhaps. But it gave me pleasure, and who cared what anyone else thought, anyway? Not that there was a crowd of people just waiting around to hear me swear. As always, the house was silent.

There used to be a clock that ticked. Tick, tick, tick. Constant noise. One day, I silenced it with a curse. And then gave it away in the next bundle of useless things that went to the place that took useless things for other people to be burdened with.

I swore again as I flicked on the light in the kitchen, only because it felt good. I knew I should give up the habit. But then I was the only one listening, and I didn't mind. And it had its uses. The sound of the words forbidden, yet effective, were a tension release.

And I was in serious need of a tension release. This was the day I both dreaded all year and dreamed about almost every night. What would the book tell me this time?

I knew it would be waiting for me where it always was on this day. I put it away each year after the day was over, and each year on this day, it found its way to the table beside my favorite chair.

If a book could choose—which I suppose somehow this book could—it picked this table beside this chair because it knew that when I opened it, I would fall asleep. Or drift away. Or leave the room, leaving my body behind.

I never could figure out exactly what happened. I had never told any of my friends what happened each year. They would think I was crazy. Or at least I worried that they would think I was crazy.

But the time was coming when I felt I would burst if I didn't tell someone what happened every year on this day, in this chair. Someone needed to know.

Perhaps Grace. Was she old enough yet? Would she think her grandmother was off her rocker? Would that matter? Knowing Grace, nothing would deter her from finding out the entire story. Made up or not, she wouldn't care.

Outside, the wind sighed, and I thought it said, "Tell her today. Before the book."

No, I said to myself. *Book first. I'm not telling Grace this now.*

But when I reached my chair, the book wasn't there. And as much as I didn't want to open it, even more, I did. I wanted to find Harry, at least in its pages.

Panicked, I wondered if perhaps the book was going to make me find it this year. A test perhaps.

But it wasn't anywhere. And it was only then that I knew how much I needed this day. I didn't dread it. I yearned for it. Because no matter what it showed me, at least I had my life back with my beloved for a moment.

Instead, now I was a lonely old woman standing in my living room, holding a cup of now cold coffee, realizing that if the book was gone, then there was nothing left in the world for me.

I should have fallen down the stairs and broken my neck. Instead, I sat down in the chair and waited.

If there was no book, something had to happen. It was Harry's birthday, after all.

Two

How much time went by as I sat in my chair waiting? I didn't know. With no ticking clock in the room and my refusal to have a cell phone so that I could spend all my time staring at it, there was no way to know.

The day remained dark and dreary, so no sunlight moved through the room to give me a clue. On most days, this was what I liked. I called it *living outside of time*.

There was a small clock in the kitchen just in case I needed to know the time of day, but otherwise, I liked the day to unfold in my own way. I went to bed in the dark and woke up in the light. Or, more accurately, I got up in the light since half the time I wasn't sleeping.

If I was lucky, I would dream, because it was always about Harry. But usually it was me in bed staring at the ceiling, watching the shifting patterns that the tree outside my window made on the ceiling when the moonlight shone through it.

Finally, my stomach growled, and I got up to make toast and get another cup of coffee. If the book does not show up today, then what should I do?

Grace had bought me a pod coffee machine so I could always have a good cup of coffee. And now that she was old enough to drive, she also kept my refrigerator stocked with my favorite foods, since she knew I didn't enjoy going to the grocery store.

I wasn't sure why I was blessed with a granddaughter like Grace, but there wasn't a day that went by when I didn't thank the good Lord for her.

When she went away to college in the fall, if I wanted to keep in touch, I would have to break down and get a cell phone. That's what she told me, and I would obey. She was my light in the world, and if that's what it took, that's what I would do.

Unlike her roving grandfather and her angry mother, who only spoke to me if necessary, as soon as Grace could find her way to my house, she was always nearby. That in itself was amazing.

But Grace also wanted to hear my stories. Ever since she was a little girl, she would follow me around and ask questions. How did she know even then that I loved to be asked questions?

Harry would say that Grace and I were a match made in heaven. "Like us," I would say back, and he would answer, "Like us," and then fold me into his arms, and I would lean against his chest, listening to his heartbeat, and be at peace. In his arms, I was content. I was home.

It had been a long time since I felt as if I was home. If I knew where Harry had gone, I would follow him. But the last time he left, he left for good. Sitting in the woods leaning against his favorite tree, he moved into the next world and left me behind.

Hunters found him the next day. I'm sure he chose a place and time where he would be easily found. But not before he let himself drift away. Did he know he was dying? He never said. Even in the night when I spoke to him in dreams, he never told me. And when I saw him in the day, he was silent.

But knowing Harry, he did what he thought was best for both of us. He knew I would want to remember him as he was, not as he was found. Now he was an actual tree in another forest. Or his body was. I could visit that tree if I wanted to. But what I wanted was Harry holding me in his arms again.

And although he promised me that could happen, I didn't see how. The closest I got to it was through the book, and now it was missing.

Some time later, I heard a knock on the door and a key in the latch. I turned, half expecting Harry to walk through the door, while knowing it couldn't be. The last time that happened was eleven years ago.

"Gammy," Grace said, "What are you doing?"

"Waiting for you?" I said, pushing myself out of the chair, pleased to be brought out of my despair by my favorite person in this world.

"I got here as soon as I could," Grace said, putting down the bag in her hand and reaching over to hug me.

Her hugs were different than Harry's had been, but just as good. Today she smelled like a bakery, and looking closely, I saw a splotch of what looked like icing on her face.

I love her face. She reminds me of an elf that I saw once in the woods. With her dark hair in a pixie cut and her dark blue eyes, she always caught the attention of everyone when she walked into a room. Not that she wanted it. But she smiled at everyone and lit up their life for a moment, anyway.

Perhaps people saw the wild in her. The girl that lives in this world, but isn't really just a girl. When she was three years old, Harry and I gave Grace an elf costume for her birthday. Within seconds, she had stripped off her everyday clothes and ran around and around the house as an elf.

We remained on the floor, surrounded by the wrapping paper she had torn off the box. Waiting, holding hands, smiling at the joy that Grace spread as she danced throughout the house. Minutes later, we felt her breath on our necks as she stood behind us. Leaning in, she whispered, "Thank you for knowing."

Did we? Perhaps Harry did. I just wanted to see her in an elf costume.

"What did you bring?" I said, gesturing to the bag.

"What do you mean?" she said, laughing. "You told me to come over and bring a cake for granddad's birthday."

"Oh yes," I laughed, knowing for sure that I hadn't.

It must have been Harry, whispering in her ear. Or the book. Or the wind. But it didn't matter. I realized this was exactly what I wanted today, and I was grateful that she had come.

And I knew what I was supposed to do. Tell Grace a story or two. But cake first. Then we would begin.

Three

Thirty minutes later, we were both staring at empty plates. We were sitting around the kitchen table Harry had made for me as a first year anniversary gift. It was really a slab of wood he had found on one of his adventures in the woods, mounted on legs from an old table he had found at a thrift shop.

Sanded and lacquered, it was beautiful, a constant reminder of Harry's love of the woods. More than once, I had tried to count the rings to see how old the tree had been, but I never succeeded. Either there were too many of them, or I got too bored with counting.

The tree table tells its own quiet story of its life through its rings and the markings of insects that had traveled through it. And now it continued to live on as a table.

I pressed my finger into the few crumbs left on the simple white plates that I love and then licked the crumbs off my finger. Rolling my eyes, I said, "Yum, that was so good."

"Maybe we could have it for lunch, too," Grace said, laughing. "It's a special day after all. And next year, I don't know if I will be in town on his birthday."

Then, seeing the look on my face that I tried to hide but failed, she quickly added, "But I will try to come home. I promise."

Sighing, I reached over and held her hand. Tiny, like her. So perfect.

"It's okay. You go to school and get everything you can from it. I'll be here whenever you come home."

And then, seeing the look on her face, which she did not hide, I added, "And I promise we'll shop for a phone this week so you can show me how to see you on it."

Her eyes lit up, making me the happiest person in the world.

We both sighed as we stared at the chocolate cake, all gooey and moist, with blue candles covered in icing lying on the plate, smelling delicious, just begging us to have another slice.

"Lunch," Grace said firmly. She stood and put the cake lid over the cake, hiding it from view. "And now, the other thing you promised me."

I stared at her, completely flummoxed. I couldn't remember promising her anything at all.

"Oh, don't try to get out of it. You said, 'Bring a cake, we'll celebrate granddad's birthday,' and then you said that you'd tell me a story or two."

So that's the way it is, I thought to myself. "You are forcing me into this, aren't you?" I said to Harry in my mind. I didn't know how Harry had managed to speak to Grace in a way that she thought it was me, but I knew he had done it.

Grace believed in magic, but she didn't make things up and was one of the most logical, full-of-common-sense people I had ever met. No wonder I loved her so. It was the same combination of talents and gifts that Harry embodied.

I believed in magic too, but only because it was forced on me. If I didn't, then I wouldn't have the book, or Harry showing up at night, or Grace in my life. Wasn't that all a form of magic?

What was magic, anyway? Was it a leaking of what was really true into the everyday world? Or was it a displacement of laws? That was the question I had asked myself years before. And answered. I had decided that I couldn't believe that the laws that run the universe could be displaced. It would be utter and complete chaos.

Not that the world wasn't always in some form of chaos. But good always wins in the end. The law of the world, or universe, had to be one of order and goodness, or it couldn't exist. That was my logical way of thinking.

Which meant I accepted that what others called magic was really the laws of the universe that we were almost always blind to. They appeared when we were willing and able to see them, but that didn't mean they weren't always working.

And Harry, blessed Harry, annoying Harry, who was always leaving me for an adventure, had opened my eyes to it. Or at least as much as I was willing to see.

Now I knew I was being forced into more acceptance of what others called magic, and I called "alternative awareness." Between Grace and Harry, I had no choice. That is, if I wanted them both to be in my life.

"Okay," I said, smiling and putting my age-spotted hands on top of her young ones once again. "Where do you want to start?"

Grace laughed and squeezed my hand. "Oh, Gammy, you are so silly. You know where to start. At the beginning, of course."

Teasing her, I said, "Of time?"

"Well, if you know that, yes, start there. But otherwise, start where you first remember being in this life."

"That could take forever."

"I have time. And if you don't finish today, we'll keep going until you do."

I knew I wouldn't win this argument, so we each got another cup of coffee and headed back to the living room. I sat in my favorite chair, and Grace sat in hers so that I could see her and yet still see the wind whipping through the trees outside.

I rarely bothered with the fire anymore, but sitting with Grace on this chilly May morning was the perfect setting to tell stories.

Leaning back in my chair, I stared into the fire, trying to decide where to begin. What was the first thing I remember? At least the first thing that I remember that was relevant to what Grace wanted.

I closed my eyes and visualized the book in my hands, and where it always began. I would follow its wisdom and tell the stories that it told me every year.

Now I was the book. At least for the day.

Four

"Well, it all began when I was almost two."

"Wait, wait. That can't be true. You remember being two?"

"Do you want to hear the story or not? And yes, I actually remember earlier than that, but that part isn't necessary for this story. What is necessary happened just before my second birthday."

Grace nodded, her blue eyes shining with delight, and settled deeper into her chair. "Okay, continue."

"Thank you, my Grace," I said, and we both laughed. It was my favorite way of addressing my beautiful granddaughter. She was definitely the queen of my world, and I didn't care that she knew it.

So I began my story about the boy named Harry who moved into the old house across the street. He was already in first grade and I was, in his eyes, still a baby. But, as he said later, I was a cute one. Except he was all boy and had very little time for the little girl that lived across the street.

As for me, I knew what I wanted the minute I saw him. I fell in love.

"At two?" Grace interrupted again.

I wagged my finger at her. "Do you want to hear the story or not?"

Closing my eyes, I went back to that day. Harry was tall for his age, or at least it seemed that way to me. But he already had those blue eyes and dark straight hair that Grace inherited, and when he looked my way, I started giggling.

I imagine he saw me, just out of diapers, curly, unruly blond hair, standing at the end of the driveway, giggling, and thought, *what a cute baby*, if he thought anything at all.

For me, it was love at first sight. Years later, Harry explained to me it was a return to loving him. He believed we had always been together, and that's why his family moved to my town, where his dad had just gotten a new job.

"Fate?" I had asked him. "No. We get to choose and we chose to be together again."

But that's implying it was all easy going after that. It wasn't. Harry was too busy for me. Maybe for anyone. There was a forest that stretched for miles behind his house, and that's where he disappeared to every chance he got.

Later, when I got to know his parents, I learned of their frustration with their son, who could rarely be found. I understood how they felt. It started that first day, and every day after that, as I watched Harry walk out the door day after day, and disappear into the woods.

But then Harry was just some kind of mystical creature to me. He was the magical boy who sometimes shared what he found in the woods. A boy who occasionally took the time to teach me how to notice the mysteries of nature.

But despite my initial feelings of love for Harry, life got in the way of being together for a lot longer than I could have thought possible.

I had just gotten to the part where my parents died and I lost Harry for years when there was a tap on the kitchen door.

"Your friend is here," Grace said, glancing at the deck outside my kitchen door. The glass door, the deck, were all gifts from Harry, so I could always see my garden, the tree he planted for me and the path into the woods.

Without looking, I knew which friend she meant. I recognized the tap.

It wasn't one of those friends that drive up in cars or walk to my house because they live just a block away. Those friends would have known not to come today. They didn't know about the book, but they knew I wanted to be alone on Harry's birthday. May 2nd every year was sacred. And they honored that.

No, this was Jay. It was a play on words because it wasn't a bluejay, it was a raven. It made me laugh to call him Jay. I don't think he appreciated me calling him Jay, but we still got along. More than got along. We were friends.

Jay had shown up the day Harry had left for good. He tapped on the glass door, head cocked to the side, and stared at me as if checking me out to see if I was the right person.

I guess I was, because he came back every day. I thought perhaps Harry had sent him to keep me company.

"Is he alone?" I asked, because sometimes Jay brought Dove. Yes, another raven. She didn't seem to mind her name, probably being too busy to care.

A few days after Jay appeared, I started leaving treats for him, and then for Dove. In return, Jay brought me little gifts. Sometimes dead mice, sometimes someone's earring. Sometimes a feather. And even though I am not a collector of things, I kept his gifts. In a box. Except for the dead animals.

"He probably wants me to go for a walk with him. Do you want to come?"

In the few hours Grace and I had been talking, the wind had stopped, and the sun had come out from behind the clouds. Jay was right. It was a good time to go for a walk. I had been sitting too long.

"Gotta get to work, Gammy," Grace replied. "Come by later for dinner?" Grace worked in a lovely diner in town, so that would be a treat.

I smiled and nodded, and Grace knew that meant I would think about it.

I grabbed my coat, hat, a scarf for my neck, and walked Grace to her car, hugging her as if it was the last time I would see her, because I knew that was always a possibility. I had missed hugging many people for the last time because I hadn't realized how fleeting life was going to be.

Not Harry, though. Before heading for the woods that day, he hugged me for a long time. I had laid my head on his shoulder for a moment, feeling his strong arms around me. We said we loved each other as we always did.

I replayed that hug countless times, glad that I had told him once again that I loved him. Not that I thought he'd forget, but it helped to know that I said it.

And so that's what I did with Grace. I told her I loved her, and she promised she'd come by to hear more stories in a few days.

Before heading down the sidewalk to the lake, I watched Grace drive away in the car her mother had given her. Jenny was a wonderful mother. Too bad she didn't seem to like me, but at least she didn't get in the way of me and Grace having a relationship.

I knew Jay would be just around the corner waiting for me to follow him. Dove probably wouldn't be there. She'd be busy doing what the females of all species seem to do. Taking care of the practical things in life.

In Dove's case, she'd be taking care of the nest that they returned to year after year, and tending to the eggs. Jay helped too. But first he'd take a walk with me. After all, he had been charged with watching over me.

I figured by the time Jay and Dove died, they would have taught one of their children to watch over me too. Maybe they'd go see Harry, and he'd get to walk with them. Or maybe they would outlive me, and then they would watch over Grace.

I checked in my pockets to make sure I had peanuts for my bird friends and set off breathing in the spring air.

It had turned out to be a lovely day, after all. Good thing I didn't fall down the stairs and break my neck. I had a mission now. Tell Grace everything. Then maybe the stairs.

Five

I was right. Jay, but not Dove, was waiting around the corner for me. He was busy pecking at a pile of leaves by the sidewalk. He didn't need to turn his head to see me. He just started strutting down the sidewalk, leading the way.

Occasionally, he'd fly ahead and wait in a tree. Sometimes he circled behind me before returning to where I was following him. Checking the territory, I assume, like a scout. Perhaps that's what I should have called him.

From the moment Jay adopted me, I felt safe when he was with me. Once, a stray dog ran aggressively towards me. I was too scared to move. Jay flew straight at that crazed dog, landed on his head, and gave him a sharp peck.

That dog, and no other dog, ever bothered me again. So walking was a genuine pleasure. Other than watching where I put my feet, there was no need to worry about my safety. I could simply enjoy the sights.

Today I purposely avoided glancing at houses as we walked. People would often see me walk by and come out to talk. Today, I didn't want to talk. I was all talked out. Besides, they always seemed to want something from me, and I didn't know what it was. Instead, I kept my eyes straight ahead, only occasionally glancing at the bobbing daffodils and peeping crocuses.

As we turned the last corner, the lake came into view. The sun, having passed the halfway point in the sky, slanted down across the lake, making it sparkle a shade of blue that I could never reproduce when I had tried to paint it.

Painting was a hobby I gave up long ago. Who needed paintings on the wall, when outside it was a changing landscape? So instead of hanging paintings, we put in windows.

There are windows everywhere in our house. People think it's weird. But to me they bring an ever-changing landscape. Birds and animals, the changing seasons, all laid out before me every day.

And on a practical side, before he died, I would often glimpse Harry as he walked away into the forest that now lay beyond our backyard, and know that he probably wouldn't be home for dinner.

Or when he was still working at his office in town, I could watch him drive away, both of us waving until he was out of sight.

I should have known something was up that last day. That day, his hug was extra long, and he stood a long time with me after he told me he loved me before he left for his walk in the woods. But I didn't know.

All of my life I had watched Harry leave, knowing he would come back. How was I to know that day he wasn't going to? How did he know?

Enough of that, I mumbled to myself, and Jay squawked at me in agreement. I brought myself back to the present and paid more attention to where I put my feet on the trail that led down to benches by the water's edge.

The benches used to be just a few feet above the water line. Now they were much further away, proof that the water table had declined. More water in the ocean, less water in our lake. Nature was going through a hard time.

Jay squawked again, oh, how I wished I had a bird language translator, and then flew away. I had to assume he was telling me he'd be back, that he just needed to check on Dove, who was most likely sitting on the eggs and getting hungry. As hard as I had looked for their nest, I never found it, although I knew it had to be nearby.

The wind was soft, and the lake gently murmured as it lapped at the shore. It was so soothing that I closed my eyes and returned to my little girl life where the love of my life lived across the street, and my mother was still alive.

It was a beautiful place to be. I could see everything just as it happened. I know memories are liars, and that every time I pulled up this memory, I changed it somehow. By wishing the outcome was different, or making it better than it actually was, I rewrote the story over and over again.

But I couldn't imagine that I made up how happy I was then. At six, I was bold and unafraid. Harry sometimes came with me on my walks or bike rides. But usually I went on my own. To me, at that time, it felt as if I had gone miles. But now I knew it wasn't far.

Harry had shown me the path he took into the woods, and sometimes I would look for him there if he wasn't with me. Back then, I never found him. But I found flowers, and acorns, and birds that hid high in the trees.

My mother constantly scolded me for having bird seeds in my pocket. But I had learned that if I was patient enough, eventually birds would come to sit by me, or eat out of my hands.

By the time I was ten, I was proficient in the forest. I'd leave my bike a few feet into the woods and head off, never worried that I wouldn't find my way back.

Harry had been lost to me by then. He had discovered girls his age. And boy stuff. To Harry, I was still the little girl who lived across the street. But I was patient. I had learned to feed birds by waiting quietly, wanting nothing. I figured someday Harry would come sit by me, in the same way that birds did.

And then tragedy struck our magically happy family. Yes, I knew bad things were possible. After all, didn't all children who ever watched a Disney movie know tragedies happened to families?

Walt Disney, with his belief in magic, also believed that children needed to know enough to be prepared for a world that took things away. I had always made my mother skip through the parts of movies where the mother died. I knew it happened. I didn't need to be reminded that bad things happened.

But then I was reminded in the most terrible way. I came home from the woods, smelling like pine, dropped my blue Schwinn bike onto the grass the way I always did, and burst through the screen door, letting it slam behind me the way I always did.

But instead of yelling at me to stop banging the screen door the way he always did, my father was sitting on the couch beside a stranger dressed like a police officer, and crying.

Life as I knew it was over that day, and a new life, one without my mother and then without my father—and finally without Harry, had begun.

Six

I took Grace up on her offer for dinner, even though I suspected she had planned more than a dinner just for me. To prepare myself, after returning from the lake, I took a quick nap. As often happens, I dreamed about Harry. In this dream, he had come home from work, and I was cooking his favorite meal. When I woke up, I was so hungry that I was ready and willing to be surprised by Grace and my friends.

Before leaving for the restaurant, I took a quick tour of the living room, looking for the book, hoping it had returned. It hadn't. So I dressed in my best but most comfortable outfit and walked to the restaurant where Grace worked, since it was just a few blocks away. I knew someone would be there to bring me home.

I had barely walked through the door before Grace spotted me and whisked me away to a table in the back where, yes, my friends were waiting for me. You'd think it was my birthday, not Harry's, the way they all smiled and hugged me.

I reminded myself that they loved Harry too, and had a right to miss him and celebrate his birthday if they wanted to. And as usual,

Grace had known it was what I really needed. Perhaps if I stopped resisting the world and all that it offered, I'd be happier.

Maybe that was what this day was all about. A missing book, a granddaughter who wanted to hear my stories—who in the world gets that lucky—and friends who understood that it would be best if I was not alone tonight.

My friends are a mixed bag. I often describe them as a bag of mixed nuts. Nobody is offended or surprised by that description. Of course, I am included in that bag. We all have learned to accept, and sometimes celebrate, our slightly salty and well-known nutty natures.

Although all of us have been out of step with the world most of our lives, it's different now because we are old women and that makes it okay to be sightly nutty. No one notices us anyway. That's what Peggy says. But in her case, she's wrong, and she knows it. Everyone notices her because that is and always has been her intention. She isn't planning to leave this world quietly.

So, even at seventy-five years old, Peggy—her name is really Peggy Sue, but she tired of people singing that song around her—wears bright purple and yellow, and dyes her long white hair with strings of color as if she was a teenager.

And loud. Lord, she can be loud. When she laughs, she sometimes sounds like a donkey braying. Does she care? No. In fact, we are all fairly certain she makes herself laugh like that on purpose.

But Peggy is the person you want around if you want to act out. Because she does. She has been known to get up in the middle of any room and start dancing, her hair swinging as wildly as her hips.

To be Peggy's friend, you have to choose whether to be embarrassed or proud. Although embarrassment sometimes popped up, most often I am proud that the most popular girl in high school found a lonely ten-year-old and befriended her.

What girl in high school does that?

I owe Peggy for so many things, not the least of which is rescuing me from drowning in depression after my mother died and my father moved us to the city.

That she ended up in the same town as me twenty years ago is a story for another time. Today she is resplendent in a bright purple jacket and an orange sweater, topped by a scarf that Isadora Duncan would have loved.

Sometimes I wonder if Peggy is Isadora returned to the world. After all, Peggy was born not long after Isadora died, having had the scarf she wore tangled in the wheels of the car she was riding in.

That's Peggy—loud, exuberant, a lover of excitement and adventure. Beside her is her exact opposite—well, not completely opposite because they both have kindness to others engraved on their hearts. If Peggy was the picture of outward energy, Faye is the quiet violet, not caring if she is noticed.

But if you did notice, and if you were her friend, you would find out that not only does Faye believe in magic, she is magic. She lives it as if it was the natural way to live in the world. I have often wondered if Faye became that way because of her name, or if she was always one with the fairies.

Grace admires and I think basically tolerates, Peggy, because Peggy is so good to me. But Faye is someone Grace loves to spend time with. Why not? An elf and a fairy would get along well, wouldn't they?

And in the middle of all of them is the throughly practical—looking exactly like one would expect a grandmother to look—Bonnie. If someone could be born looking like a grandmother, it would be Bonnie. It's almost as if she had been sixty forever.

The thing is, she isn't anyone's grandmother. Instead, she is anyone's grandmother who will have her. A retired, never married school teacher, there is always someone who hugs her as if she were their grandmother. Everyone loves Bonnie. Maybe she isn't part of the bag of nuts that we are. She is the bag itself, holding us all together.

How I met each of these women are some stories I read in the book each year. And I am sure that part of the reason Grace got them all here was because she wanted to hear another story or two from at least one of them.

My suspicions were confirmed when, after serving us all dinner and making sure our desserts were ordered, Grace declared herself off work and pulled up a chair and said, "Tell me again how you all met?"

Seven

Faye dipped her head, trying to disappear. Bonnie looked around the room for someone to go say hello to, so I sighed and pointed to Peggy, who perked up even more, if that was possible.

Given the life Peggy lived, I had to admire that she never seemed to let it dim her down. Other people, me included, would have been tempted to turn off the world and retreat.

What am I thinking? That's exactly what I do all the time, and if it weren't for this mixed bag of nuts I call friends, I would never come out of my cave. Even today, that's what would have happened.

But, instead of a day alone, reviewing the book that only works once a year, I am out at dinner with friends, after having a lovely walk with Jay, and spending most of the day with Grace. Not a normal Harry's birthday at all.

Peggy smiled and said, "I'll go first."

Grace clapped her hands with glee. She said, "Just a minute," and got up, taking the bill with her, dismissing our protests, saying it was her birthday present to Harry.

When she returned, she brought another tea for Faye, and poured us all another cup of coffee. Sitting down, she pointed at Peggy and said, "Now you can begin."

Peggy laughed and, turning to me, said, "How did you end up with this delightful creature?"

"I ask myself that all the time," I replied.

Although Grace blushed, she was not deterred. She just gave Peggy the look she often gives me when I haven't eaten enough, or have gotten up late, or haven't remembered to brush my hair.

Grace is a demanding elf, but it's always in our best interests. This is something she often reminds anyone she is bossing around.

Peggy shifted in her seat, removed a strand of purple hair from her red jacket, leaned forward, and did what Grace had demanded. She began.

She began with how she found me crying, huddled behind a garbage bin behind the school. She could have walked on by. I had tried to hide from her when I saw her coming. I knew who she was. Who didn't know Peggy Sue Brannon? She was the head cheerleader, beautiful, and loud. No one could miss her.

Dad had moved us out of our house, away from the woods, away from Harry, and brought us to the city across the country, as far away from home as he could get. Even as a girl, I understood why. He couldn't stand to be around anything that reminded him of his wife. That included me.

But he couldn't get rid of me, so he took me along with him as he shed his past life, and became someone I didn't know. I understood the reason, but it didn't make it hurt less.

I was huddled behind the garbage bins, crying for my mother and my father, for my home, for Harry, for the animals and trees that had been my friends in the woods.

Not only did I hate the city, but I was positive that the city hated me. The kids in class certainly seemed to. They either ignored me, or made fun of how small I was, how shy, how stupid I was in school, and how I didn't fit into their world. I preferred the ignoring, but it was more often bullying, so I had found many places to hide.

But Peggy found me that day, and didn't tolerate it for a minute. "Come out from behind there, girl," she said. Even then, no one didn't do what Peggy asked of them.

I shuffled out. My dress was dirty, my hair a long curly matted mess, and I am sure I smelled. Not just because of the garbage bin, but because I often forgot to take a bath at night, burying myself instead in a book, letting it take me out of the world I had found myself in.

To Peggy's credit, she didn't ask why I was a mess. All she said was, "That's enough of that."

And it was. She walked me home, studied the mess that the house was in, made me take a shower while she made dinner from what she found in the refrigerator. As we ate, she listened to my pathetic little story and said again, "That's enough of that."

What I didn't know until years later was that she cried all the way home. That her heart was broken. But even then, she knew that showing me pity would not help. What did help is what she told her parents, who came over to the house while I was asleep and talked to my dad.

Although he never became the father I had known before, he hired someone to clean the house, and prepare meals for me, and him if he came home at night.

All of that meant that I had clean clothes, combed hair, was well fed, and smelled nice. But what really changed everything was that Peggy Sue Brannon walked me to school every morning before crossing the street to go to the high school.

I was never bullied or ignored again.

Grace listened to the story. Her eyes filled with tears and she reached over to hold my hand. We all remained silent until Peggy said, "That's enough of that!"

And it was. Enough of that story. I never wanted to hear it again. I never wanted Grace to feel sorry for me. It occurred to me then that perhaps that was why the book hadn't shown up today. Eleven years of mourning was enough. As Peggy said. "That's enough of that."

Thank you, Peggy," Grace said as she hugged her.

When I glanced at Peggy, I saw she had tears in her eyes, too. I could have told Grace more of Peggy's story, how she chose men who didn't know how to love her, lost her parents too early, and didn't have the children she always wanted. But I wouldn't. Because Peggy was a constant reminder that no matter what, life was to be lived out loud.

And that is the message for today, I decided. What that meant for me, I didn't know. All I knew was that once again life had turned, and it would be different from now on. It was time to come out from behind the garbage bin.

As we said our goodbyes to Grace, she reminded me she still wanted to hear how I met Faye and Bonnie, and how Peggy ended up back in my hometown. I nodded and said those stories were for another day.

Bonnie drove me home. I fell asleep the minute I pulled the covers up over me. It was the best sleep I had in ages. And didn't dream of Harry. For once.

Eight

The next morning, the book was still not there, but Grace was—with Faye. I had woken up to the smell of coffee and a whistling kettle. As I glanced at the clock by my bed, I was shocked to discover that I had slept in. I couldn't remember the last time that had happened.

Even though I had practically fallen into bed the night before, I had at least laid out clothes. Habits work in our favor sometimes, so I pulled them on as quickly as possible. I could hear the elf and fairy giggling downstairs, and I wanted to be part of whatever was going on.

That's new, I said to myself as I checked the old lady's face in the mirror and brushed her hair. The old lady's face wasn't new. I had been looking at that face for years and even though I barely recognized her, I reluctantly accepted that it was me.

What was new was that I couldn't wait to get downstairs. And today I knew for sure I didn't want to fall down the stairs and break my neck. Today I held on tightly to the bannister as I carefully put one foot in front of the other, wondering for a moment if I should move to some place easier to live in.

But I put that thought away. For now, anyway.

Grace and Faye were in the kitchen, sitting around the tree table. That's what Faye always called it, and of course it was. Trees live on forever in many forms, as Harry had reminded me, as he installed the table in the kitchen.

"Too bad we don't," I had mumbled, thinking back to my mother and so many of my friends who had died.

"Oh, but we do," Harry had said, gathering me into his arms and resting his chin on my head. I pretended not to agree with him, just to keep him comforting me. I knew what he said was true, but I still missed my mother, even after all these years.

"You okay, Gammy?" Grace asked. I had come to a full stop inside the door because, for the moment, I had felt Harry's arms around me.

"Just waking up," I responded, knowing that neither Grace nor Faye believed me.

Bringing myself back to the present, I realized that there was a place setting for me, with a steaming cup of coffee beside it. And a plate with my favorite morning treat, a chocolate croissant.

"Faye's idea," Grace said when she saw my eyes light up. I knew better than that. I knew it was Grace, but I hugged Faye for it anyway. She winked at me, and I tipped my head. We old people do have secrets, after all.

Of all my friends, it was Faye who I have known the longest. And it was because of Faye that I returned to my hometown after my father died and left me the house he never sold.

"He couldn't bring himself to do it," his attorney had told me at his funeral.

That dad had been thinking of me surprised me, even though I knew it shouldn't have. But even though I knew dad still loved me, we had never reconnected. Never returned to our talks about almost anything. Never went to visit a garden again. Never read books together. We never laughed together again at a silly cartoon on a Saturday morning, with me snuggled up to him, smelling the Old Spice cologne that he loved to wear. A scent that would linger with me all day long.

The drunk driver, a sixteen-year-old boy and a car filled with teenagers that had crashed into my mother's car, killing her instantly, had taken away our entire life. Changed my dad into a closed-off, bitter, but very successful business executive, instead of a father who always had time for his strange daughter.

He had been a father who had always listened to my explanations of magic as if he believed them. Perhaps he had. But those kinds of discussions, or any discussion that didn't involve what he was required to do as the father of a ten-year-old girl who lost her mother, did not happen. That life was gone, and a new life had begun.

It was Harry and Faye who were there for me until I was moved away from everything I loved. And it was Faye who convinced me to come back when she heard dad had given the house to me.

Faye and I had stayed in touch with letters and sometimes phone calls. They petered out by the time we both went off to college, but I still knew how to find Faye if I needed to, and she checked in with me once in a while.

So when dad died, and I was trying to decide what to do with an old house in my hometown, it was Faye who said, "Come home."

I was going to say no, but when she added, "Harry sometimes comes to town," I said yes.

Unlike Faye, Harry had not stayed in touch. I only found out that his parents died through Faye. I wrote him, telling him how sorry I was, but he didn't respond. Through Faye, I learned he had gone off to school, majored in environmental science and taken a job that moved him from one forest to another in all parts of the world.

One day, while shopping for a new book to read, I had moved to my favorite section of the local bookstore, and saw a book with his name on it. Harry Lang. Thinking that it was a coincidence that there were two Harry Langs—both of whom loved the forest—I opened the book to the first page and read about this one.

It was my Harry. I was so shocked that I collapsed to the floor, the book open on my knees, and stared at it. My Harry, the one person I tried to forget but never could, had written a book. And it was in the bookstore, waiting for me. That was how it felt, anyway.

Sitting on the floor, I cried. The owner found me there. I guess a few people had seen me and told her that a strange woman was sobbing over a book. The owner helped me to my feet, hugged me, gave me the book, and told me to come back if I wanted to talk about it.

Kindness is not as rare as one might think. Especially given the constant, intense focus on what is wrong in the world, which are many, many things. But kindness is present in everyone. Or almost everyone.

On that day, the book owners' kindness helped me rally. Recover. Remind myself that Harry didn't care about me, and I needed to get on with my life.

And that's exactly what I did. Until dad died, and Faye called. And that began the second turning of my life.

Nine

"Do you want to go shopping with me, Gammy?" Grace asked after Faye had gone home to take care of her cats. Faye didn't really need to take care of them. If anything, they took care of her, but she was giving me another morning to spend just with Grace.

Faye knew I dreaded Grace leaving to go to the university in the fall. And if that wasn't bad enough, Grace would also be gone a huge hunk of the summer. That meant I wouldn't have much more time with her before she became someone else. She'd be free to choose a new version of herself, and that was a good thing.

Maybe the new Grace would also love me, but it was also possible that she wouldn't. The prospect terrified me. At the same time, I was happy for Grace. Yes, it was possible to hold two opposing ideas at the same time. In this case, being terrified and happy for the same reason.

The reason Grace would be gone for most of the summer was because she was going to be working at a summer camp. It was the same one she had always gone to as a camper for the last ten years. Harry and I had paid for the camp, and Jenny reluctantly let her go, recognizing that just because she didn't love the outdoors herself, her daughter did.

I didn't know exactly what Grace would be doing, but I knew that working at the camp would be perfect for her. The helping kids part. And the woods. Always the woods, it was where the elf in Grace really came alive.

Harry had often taken Grace with him into the woods and shown her its treasures. He often told me stories of what Grace already knew, and how he'd have to keep close watch on her, or she would wander off following a deer, or rabbit, or even a fox. None of them seemed to mind. In fact, I am sure they invited her to follow.

I was always grateful that when Harry took Grace with him to the woods, he would tell me where they were going so I wouldn't panic looking for her. And Harry was always careful to get her home in time to get Grace cleaned up before Jenny arrived to take her home.

Sometimes Grace came home from the woods so filthy that we had to give her a bath before Jenny got there. But we always delivered a clean, happy child back to her mother.

Jenny hated the woods. And didn't much care for me either. She loved her dad, despite his constant absences. Me, the one who was always there for her, not so much.

When Grace asked me if I wanted to go shopping with her, I was going to say "no." It was on the tip of my tongue. That was my habit, to say no. But before the words fell out of my mouth, I remembered that yesterday I had decided that the book and Harry were trying to tell me I had entered another phase of life. There was no point in resisting it. It was happening with or without my permission and participation.

So instead of saying no, as I always did when Grace asked me to go shopping, I said yes. Grace had already put on her sweater in anticipation of going alone, so my yes startled her. Recovering quickly, she smiled, rushed to the closet and got my old coat, gloves, and hat.

"I don't need all that, Grace," I laughed, as she tried to help me put them all on.

Seeing her face, I added, "What a wonderful mother you will make someday, Grace."

Grace laughed at herself standing there with mittens, a hat, and a winter coat when outside the sun was shining, and a warm breeze was drifting through the window.

"I know we are going grocery shopping, but could we also go to the mall and get me a new coat?"

Grace stared at me as if I had grown two heads, but again recovered quickly. Maybe she remembered me from before Harry died when I was much more adventurous. I barely remembered that woman, but I was determined to find her again, and that started with a few new clothes.

"And a phone," I added. "I need a phone."

Ten

M any long hours later, Grace and I returned home. Both of us were exhausted. Grace from trying to help me navigate strange stores and strange experiences, and me from being in the middle of a life change and all that meant.

I wonder why no one talks about the old age crisis, when so much attention is given to the middle age crisis. Sometime in middle age, everyone realizes they are facing the second half of their life, and there is no going back. In response, almost everyone acts out in some way. Sometimes that acting out works in their favor, and often it doesn't.

The old age crisis exists too, but it's not so dramatic. Or perhaps it is, but because we are more invisible, no one notices. Or maybe it's because we are too tired to make a fuss about it. And of course there are fewer of us that make it that far. We know it is something to be grateful for, but we often need to be reminded of that fact when we are constantly saying goodbye to friends and family as they die and leave us.

I knew I was in the middle of my personal old age crisis. How much time I have left, I don't know. Who does? But at least I see that the door that takes me out of this world into the next is much, much closer. In fact, I see it is cracked open the tiniest bit.

Which means things—me included—had to change, because I had lived again. I would start this new phase of life with dignity and more happiness. Instead of closing down, I was going to open up. Going shopping with Grace was the beginning of the plan.

But the noise and crowds and the phone store with all its choices were too much. Poor Grace had to listen to my quiet, and not so quiet, curses as I tried to understand what the guy at the phone store was saying to me. It was total gibberish. I'm positive he was speaking another language.

Finally, I bought the phone Grace told me to buy, promising me she would show me how to use it later. I was too exhausted to argue. Besides, Grace was an excellent teacher, and I needed that phone to become part of the world again.

I imagine the phone guy had to take a long break after dealing with me. "So sorry," I said to him as we left the store. He waved it away as if it was nothing, but I knew it wasn't.

I needed to stop acting out this way, especially around Grace. I embarrassed her. She said I didn't, but I knew she had been cringing, wondering why she had agreed to any of it.

Exhausted from shopping and my own behavior, I lay down on the couch. Through barely open eyes, I watched Grace put the groceries away. Within minutes I had drifted off, only vaguely aware that Grace had put a cover over me and said she'd see me later.

This time I did dream. The kind of dream that Faye called an out-of-body experience. I could see myself lying on the couch, but at the same time, I was in a big, beautiful grassy meadow. And young again. Well, at least I felt young. Free, no aches, no pains.

I didn't recognize the meadow, but it reminded me of my childhood before the death of my mother. Seeing a clump of trees in the distance, I moved in that direction, getting there in record time because I didn't have to walk. I could fly.

Once inside the circle of trees, I noticed a small brook bubbling out of the ground. It was cool and quiet within this family of trees. Leaves whispered together. A lizard sunned himself by the brook, and the cutest rabbit ever peeked at me from under the tangle of a raspberry bush.

Just across the brook, a mockingbird sang a variety of songs. I knew he was letting me see it was him, so I could admire how talented he was. When I thanked him for the songs, he cocked his head and sang another song sounding just like a wren.

As I sat down on a handy rock, I could feel the coolness of it against the back of my bare legs. And then Harry was there. Not the grown-up Harry, the twelve-year-old boy, and then I knew where we were.

We were in our own little world, the one that existed before a crazed world filled with instant gratification, social media and constant noise became the normal. The one we knew together before my mom died.

For a long moment, everything was perfect. Then I woke up, returning to my body. But before I did, I heard Harry tell me he was happy about the decisions I had made that day.

Afterwards, I lay on the couch staring at the ceiling, wishing I could return to that grove of trees and that lifetime. But they were over. All my memories are just that, memories.

It was time to make some new ones. Sitting up, I reached over and opened the book Grace had made for me when she was twelve for an art project in school. She had taken some of my favorite sayings and put them all in one place along with a sketch for each one. Then she bound it together and gave it to me on my birthday.

I told her it was the best birthday present ever. When I needed inspiration, I would open it up, read the quote, and admire the little sketch that Grace always added to it.

The one I opened to this time couldn't have been more perfect. It was an illustration of a budding tree on a hill in front of a rising sun. Or was it a setting sun? The quote was from Pope Paul VI.

"Somebody should tell us, right at the start of our lives, that we are dying. Then we might live life to the limit, every minute of every day. Do it! I say. Whatever you want to do, do it now! There are only so many tomorrows."

So true, I said to myself. But for me, the question was, what did I want to do? And who did I want to do it with?

I knew the answer to the second part of the question, and they were the same people who could help me figure out the first. Using my land line—I still didn't know how to use that shiny phone sitting on the tree table—I called Bonnie, Faye, and Peggy.

They all answered the same way. "Of course. I'll be there."

I knew that the next day Grace would be on a day trip with her mother, so we'd have the whole day to plan our adventure together. We'd tell Grace about it once we figured out what it was and got it going.

This needed to be the plan of four old and older women who had decided to live out loud.

I was beginning to be very grateful that the book of memories was missing.

Eleven

The next day was bright and sunny, and I found myself humming as I dressed and headed downstairs. It was so unusual for me to be doing anything other than cursing and trying to decide whether or not to fall down the stairs, that I almost looked around for the person who was humming.

You used to sing all the time, I reminded myself, so I kept on humming and could feel the vibrations in my heart loosening things. I stopped when I could feel tears coming on. That was enough of that for now.

As I pulled out plates and rooted around for the deck of cards we had always used, I realized that I hadn't had my friends over to my house to play cards and talk for over eleven years.

The last time they had been in my house together was for Harry's wake. I was so numb that day that I barely remember what happened. I just knew they, and it seemed the whole village, were there, and then they were gone, leaving me with so much food in the refrigerator that I took most of it back to the woods and dumped it for any animals who might be hungry.

It had been a cold, bitter day, but I had trudged out there with my slippers and robe on, carrying one casserole after another. I had seen Jay that day, but didn't know he and Dove had been sent to watch over me, so I ignored them. I ignored everything for a long time.

Even Jenny had come to check in on me, but her grief over losing her father pushed her away even further from me, and she stopped coming. Grace had been a precocious seven-year-old, so she did her best to tell her Gammy that it would be okay, but even she couldn't convince me it would be.

At seven, Grace hadn't fully realized that her granddad would never take her into the woods with him again. And when Harry was alive, he was the reason she came to the house. Once she figured out that everything was different, and it wasn't okay, it was a few years before she started calling me, asking if she could spend the afternoon with me.

At first, I thought Jenny had put her up to it, but that wasn't the case at all. I eventually accepted that Grace actually wanted to see me. She wanted to share what she was learning in school. She never talked about her home life, probably aware that it wouldn't be fair to her mother.

It was just her and Jenny, and they both seemed happy about that. Jenny was an amazing mother. I am sure she tried to do everything differently than what I did with her, but my guess was, we were much more alike than Jenny would ever admit.

As for Grace's father, Jenny was the only person who knew who he was, and she wasn't telling. When Jenny came home from the university, having graduated with honors, she informed us she was pregnant, and she was keeping the child.

Harry and I asked if she wanted to come home. We had room. We'd love to have her. Jenny said she could manage on her own, and she had. I knew very little of her life, even though we lived in the same town.

But I was grateful that even though Jenny didn't like me, she had never come between me and Grace. I'm sure I would have followed Harry out that door already if it wasn't for Grace.

When she came to my house, dropped off by her mother, who only waved from the car, I gave Grace my full attention, such as it was. We baked cookies together and drank hot chocolate while she told me what she learned in school.

Like her mother, Grace was a whiz at learning. She soaked everything up, digested it, and then clearly explained what she had learned. Grace was the one who explained to me how the term "wake" applied to something that seemed to me to not be something you'd want to be awake for.

She said it was that the term "wake" originally referred to a late-night prayer vigil, where mourners would keep watch over their dead until they were buried.

When I asked her how long that had been going on, she said the tradition of holding a funeral wake was centuries old, and it's believed that the first funeral wake took place in Ireland in the 6th century.

The wake was held to allow the friends and family of the deceased to say goodbye, and it gradually spread to other parts of the world.

Although I thought the word "wake" was used because you'd have to be awake to hold a prayer vigil, she said it was also because, at the time, unknown diseases had plagued the countryside causing some people to appear to be dead, but as the family began to mourn, they would awaken.

Grace confided to me that was what she thought might happen to her granddad. As a child, she didn't know that his body was gone when we held our wake, but I understood what she meant. I too had wished that somehow he would return and say it was all a mistake.

That Harry still does return to see me is not the same. There are no hugs or Sunday morning snuggles. No shared dinners or walks in the woods. Still, it is better than nothing, and I am grateful. I only worry that Harry is hanging around out of a sense of duty, and he really should be walking toward the light.

Someday I need to ask Grace if Harry speaks to her. I imagine he does, but she likes to keep those kinds of things private, and might never tell me if I don't ask. After all, it's weird, isn't it? Perhaps it's all a figment of my imagination, or some kind of brain disease. But if that was the case, I've had it my entire life.

It took me a while to figure out where the set of cards we used had gone to, and in the process, I noticed how much of the house had become cluttered and was too dark. It was an old house to start with. Now it was looking even more decrepit than me.

Don't worry, I said to it, as I heard the car door slam and knew it was my friends arriving. *I'll do something with you too, but first, we need to decide what I want to do with myself.* I swear the house shivered. With delight, I hoped.

Peggy knew enough not to bother to ring the doorbell or knock. She opened the door and belted out, "Yahoo, anybody home?"

Not waiting for my reply, she walked in and said, "Oh, my."

Seeing me standing in the kitchen door, she said, "Did I say that out loud?"

I laughed. "You know you did, and you did it on purpose." I knew she was referring to the state of the house, and me too.

Bonnie and Faye had followed her into the house, and ignoring us, headed to the kitchen to get coffee and tea. I knew they felt the same way as Peggy, and I silently promised the house again to attend to its needs. After me, of course.

After eating what was left of Harry's birthday cake—Peggy choosing to lick her plate as she laughed at us, shaking our heads at her—we settled at the tree table to play a game of cards. Bonnie had a notebook by her. We knew she would take notes as we discussed what needed to finally be discussed.

The cards had always simply been a way to occupy our hands as we talked about everything under the sun. Today we would talk about what to do with me. I didn't need to ask. Knowing my friends, they had been waiting for eleven years for me to make this decision.

All I knew was I wanted to do something that would mean something. Make a difference to someone. That was what I decided I wanted to do. But what?

Then Bonnie did what she did so well. She started asking questions, and one thing led to another, and I was telling about where my father took us, and what I did with my life until my father died and Faye brought me home.

Twelve

I t took me a few moments before I could answer Bonnie's question about what had happened after my mom died. They already knew a little, especially since it was when I met Peggy.

But I figured a review wouldn't hurt, and then we could move on. So I gave them the condensed, rinsed out version of most of the drama. I told them how, after mom died, dad had decided to get as far away from our home as possible. Perhaps he had thought that the more miles he put between us and the house on the quiet street in a small village in Pennsylvania, the better.

So he took us away from the seasons and from the quiet of our lives to a suburb outside of Los Angeles. There we found heat, noise, and constant blue skies, except for a few months when it rained.

At that time, California was considered paradise, and I suppose it was. But not for me. It was not at all what I was expecting. I had only seen pictures of Southern California, and the reality of it was much different.

When my dad told me we were moving to a suburb of Los Angeles, I thought a suburb meant the same thing in California as it did where we lived in Pennsylvania. Perhaps miles between each town filled with trees and meadows. In Los Angeles, every suburb blended into the next. Even in 1964, it was impossible to discern where one town ended and another began.

Dad drove the entire way as if he were a man on a mission, which of course he was. He barely spoke, both of us grieving. I was too young to know what to say, and dad was too broken.

Everything we owned, except what we left behind in the house because he couldn't deal with it, was in a blue, almost new Pontiac LeMans. I overheard Dad tell our neighbor that he had gotten it for a song because he knew the manager of the one dealership in town, and the car had been driven by the sales team for a few months. It was used, but new.

I think dad liked the symbolism of it, even if he wouldn't have mentioned it. We were used, but new. At least, that was his plan. A new life for both of us. And it was. Somehow, he packed everything we needed into that car with a tiny trunk. I sat in the back seat, wedged between boxes and suitcases. In the front seat, instead of mom, there were more boxes and the food we would eat along the way to save money.

Surrounded by boxes and suitcases, I sulked, cried, slept, and watched the scenery go by, thinking that my mother would never find me since we were going too far away. And the truth is, she never showed up in my room again as a shadowy figure, smiling at me the way she used to.

As we stepped into the car, the house locked and the keys handed to a real estate agent who said he'd rent it for us, Harry walked across the street to say goodbye to me.

For me, it was the end of the world. Harry was much more casual about our parting. After all, I was only one of his friends then, not the love of his life. He hugged me goodbye and promised me we'd see each other again. But I didn't believe him.

Riding across America that week, sometimes sleeping in the car, sometimes in cheap motels, I was heartbroken over everything. Nothing was ever going to be right again. And it wasn't for a very long time.

Once we crossed the border into California, the song "California Here We Come" popped into my head, would not leave, and kept me awake. So instead of sleeping, I watched the scenery go by. Dad kept driving, even after it got dark. I suppose he just wanted it to be over.

Once I looked to my left, and I saw fires burning by the side of the road. For years afterward, I looked for what those fires had been. I never figured it out. Perhaps they were a symbol of where I thought we were going. We had left the heaven I knew and were heading into hell.

When dad drifted, the car would hit some kind of bump on the road, and he would pull himself straight again. I was too young to realize that he was probably so tired that he was falling asleep. If I had known, I would have been even more terrified.

With the song playing in my head, I was wide awake as we crested a hill and saw what was laid out in front of us. In the middle of all that blackness was a sprawling display of lights that seemed to go on forever. I never forgot that image; even today, I can see it exactly as I saw it for the first time.

I know I gasped. I think dad did too. In my wildest imagination, I could not have imagined so many lights spread out as far as I could see. It was massive. All I wanted to do at that moment was go home. What I saw before me was a nightmare.

I think dad felt the same way, even though he said nothing. Instead, he found us a motel, and we staggered to bed. The next morning, I opened the door of the motel and once again gasped. The sun was so bright, I had to squint. I could see our car in the parking lot, and beyond it were stores, cars, and weird trees stuck up like umbrellas, providing no shade from the heat.

Beside the motel door, there was a small garden plot containing the weirdest-looking plant I had ever seen. I found out later that it was called a Bird of Paradise. But at the time, it confirmed to me that we had arrived on another planet, and I knew I was not going to like it.

Thirteen

By the time I reached that point in the story, everyone was restless, including me. They had all heard some of it before, so I didn't know why I had to repeat it all again, but Bonnie said they needed to hear everything. I figured what she really meant was that she wanted me to get it all out, so I'd stop drowning myself in the past.

"Let's move a little before continuing," Faye said. We all groaned. Faye went to yoga a few days a week, and I knew for a fact that she did breathing and meditation exercises every day. So, for Faye, moving a little would be fun. The rest of us, not so much.

But we agreed, because she was right. Getting old was no excuse for not being flexible, even though I was no longer flexible by any stretch of the imagination in any part of my life. I was rigid in my sorrow and guilt for what I had done. That part I hadn't gotten to yet in the story, and I wasn't looking forward to talking about it.

After doing a few of what Faye called simple exercises that, to me, felt like I was in Navy Seal training, we decided to sit in the living room instead of the kitchen to finish our talk. Although no one else was talking, I was the one who had to tell her story, and for a minute I was mad about that. Then I remembered they were there for me, and got over myself.

Peggy had opened all the blinds in the living room, so more light streamed in, reminding me why I kept them closed most of the time. The light revealed how old and tired-looking the room looked. I pretended to myself that I didn't notice, so I wouldn't feel guilty about letting the house as well as myself go, and I started the story again.

Dad and I had arrived in Los Angeles at the beginning of the summer, so school was over until the fall. Dad had a job lined up already, which meant he had to figure out what to do with me. We were staying in a small apartment building and I convinced him to just tell the neighbors to keep an eye on me, because I would be fine on my own.

And I was really. At first I stayed in the apartment all day, and at least once a day the next-door neighbor, a woman I thought was ancient at the time even though I realized later she was only in her fifties, would knock on the door, and bring me something to eat.

Eventually I went outside, and explored the neighborhood, and met some kids living in the building. After that, although I wasn't happy, I wasn't as sad as I had been before. Dad and I fell into a routine that agreed with us, both of us grieving, but doing it in our own way.

On the weekends, dad would take us to the beach. He'd erect an umbrella, sit in his chair and read, while I built sand castles and swam in the ocean. By the end of the summer, my hair was almost white and anything not covered by my bathing suit was nut brown. We both grew a little happier that summer because of the beach.

But of course, summer had to end, and I had to go to school. All summer, I was only slightly worried about going to a strange school because I knew the kids in the neighborhood and figured I would be okay.

But then we moved away from the helpful neighbor, and the friends I had made, into a small duplex, and all of that happiness we had built up dropped away. I knew nobody. The landlord was mean, and the couple on the other side of the wall in the duplex were loud and dirty.

If I would have known how terrible school would be until Peggy found me behind the garbage bin, I would have tried to convince dad I didn't need to go to school. It wouldn't have worked, but I would have tried. Life in the duplex was miserable, too. And dad was gone even more than before.

However, once Peggy arrived in my life, I fell into a routine that I could handle. Once the bullying stopped, school work was easy for me, and with Peggy's expert guidance about people, I avoided much of the craziness that seemed to attack most teenagers.

Over the years I didn't have many friends, other than Peggy, but I had discovered theater and books. The combination of those two things meant I always had something to do that I loved.

By the time Peggy graduated and headed to UCLA, I was doing okay. A nicer neighbor moved next door, and the landlord stopped bugging us because I took care of the grounds around the duplex for him. Well, it wasn't for him, it was for me. I wanted a pretty place to live.

Peggy still checked in on me, and even though she had graduated from UCLA by the time I was ready for school, I decided to go there, too. I already knew the campus well because sometimes Peggy would pick me up from school and take me to Westwood, or to concerts at the University.

And it was because of Peggy that I got into UCLA. She helped me with the application and I think pulled a few strings. Although only six years older than me, Peggy had become an older sister and mother wrapped into one person. Dad had handed my upbringing over to her more and more while he became more and more distant.

By the time I started dating, it was Peggy who checked out the boy, and sometimes made us go on a double date with her. I doubt her boyfriends liked that, but even then Peggy didn't care what other people thought.

My life had settled into a pleasant, and sometimes happy, rhythm. Until one day Peggy eloped with her first husband. I was the only one at her "wedding" and I cried a thousand tears after it was over, as she left to go live in another city.

But we kept in touch. She came to my graduation, dragging my dad with her. It was Peggy who helped me get a job as a broker at the Merrill Lynch office in downtown Los Angeles. By then, I was a thoroughly modern city girl. I loved my job. I loved my little apartment that overlooked the city. I had long ago put Harry and the woods out of my head.

By then, I couldn't imagine myself living any other life. I could walk to the theatre from my apartment, and spent the quiet weekends with books and a few friends I had made from work and the networking I did to get business.

I saw my father a few times a year, mostly on holidays. Although he had a few long-term relationships, he never married again. What he had wanted for both of us came true. We were used, but new.

When I got married to one of the other brokers at the firm, my father and Peggy came to the wedding. Truth be told, I barely remember that wedding. I barely remember that man either. When we divorced a few years later, neither one of us was sad about it.

I heard he married again and had twin boys. I was happy for him.

Fourteen

"And then your dad died," Faye said, prompting me to begin again.

After talking about my marriage, I stopped talking. Thinking back on my time in California and Los Angeles had taken me into another world. Because that was what it was. I had started out broken from my mother's death, but then I found a few friends.

I went to college and loved the entire experience from beginning to end. Afterwards, I had worked in a profession I was good at, even though I wasn't in love with it. Along the way, I got married and divorced.

Looking back, I realized that all of that happened within a very short period of time. Did it have any bearing at all on what happened later? I filed that question away for another time. We'd eventually get to that.

One thing Los Angeles didn't have was the kind of magic I had experienced with Harry. I didn't see fairies in the woods or catch an elf sitting in my mother's flower pot. Flowers didn't sing to me, and trees didn't bend so I could reach an apple. Birds didn't sit in my hands to eat.

All those things that had happened before we moved were things I never told anyone about. They belonged to Harry, me, and my mom. And since that life was over, I had tidied them up, packed them away, and cataloged all those memories as childhood fantasies.

In college, I learned about perception biases and realized I had seen and experienced those things because Harry told me to see them, and I had agreed with him. In California, I told myself to grow up and leave all those fantasies behind, so I did. So if Harry's kind of magic existed in downtown Los Angeles, it was invisible to me.

But I'd been happy there. Los Angeles had its own kind of magic. I lived a few blocks from the theater, so I could walk there on the weekends, getting in line for tickets they gave away after everyone was seated. There was always someone who didn't show up. Afterwards, I sometimes went out with the actors I had met in the theatre department at UCLA.

During the week, I could walk to work. I enjoyed walking the pathways through buildings and hearing the sounds of the city early in the morning. I lived within walking distance of many foreign lands. China, Japan, and Korea had their own sections of downtown. And then on the weekends, because at the time very few people lived downtown, it became a quiet place where I could read, order food in, or eat out with the friends that I had made who came to see me.

Yes, I was very happy again. It was a different kind of happiness from the happiness I had before we moved to California, but I was content. But then, as Faye said, my dad died, and it was as if a cleaver fell into my life and chopped it in half again.

One day I was a city girl, and the next I had to once again leave everything I loved and start over. And even though it was my choice this time, it didn't hurt any less. The only difference was that this time I wasn't mad at my mom for dying; I was mad at my dad for leaving me again.

I suppose I had always thought that dad and I would make up some day. But we never did. We rarely saw each other. His birthday, my birthday, my wedding, and sometimes we met on mom's birthday. Not for long. Just long enough to have lunch together, maybe take a walk. Then a quick hug and goodbye, and it would be over.

And even though we had seen each other months before, he kept it from me that he was dying. It turned out that he had known even then. I suppose dad didn't want to deal with the feelings that might have come up. And he was probably right. Despite being happy, I had never stopped grieving for my mom and my life across the street from Harry and blaming him for taking me away.

When the attorney told me that dad had left the house in Pennsylvania to me, I knew what dad had done. He was trying to make up for what had happened, and that only made me grieve more. Couldn't he have talked to me about it?

But as Faye said later, when I was whining about it, I was also responsible for the lack of communication. I could have brought up my feelings. It was both our faults. Or neither of our faults. It's just the way it was.

I was so convinced by Faye that it was the right thing to do that I quit my job, said goodbye to my friends, and went home. It was just as hard to reverse my journey as it was to leave in the first place.

The glitter, newness, noise, and lights of Los Angeles had become my reality. However, I had talked myself into being excited about returning. In my mind's eye, my tiny home town was quaint and quiet, and I couldn't wait to return to it.

However, as shocking as moving to California was, coming home was just as shocking. It was quiet, all right. Too quiet. And the house was not quaint.

It barely resembled the home I had grown up in. Years of tenants and neglect had turned it into a sagging old home. The garden we had loved was grown over. Weeds grew instead of a lawn, and the street that seemed so wide before had somehow become narrow and full of potholes.

Harry, of course, had moved away long before, so I didn't actually think I would see him again. And I didn't. But I was still sad that he wasn't there, and I hoped that what Faye had said about him visiting was true. But maybe she was just making it up to get me to come home. However, the woods were still there, and it was the only thing that seemed to have improved while I was gone.

To return home, I drove myself across the country this time. All my belongings were packed in the car, just as they had been before. But this time, I had money. Money I had saved the few years I had worked at Merrill Lynch and the money my father's insurance gave me. It was enough to last me a lifetime if I was careful.

Which meant I had choices. Dad had given me choices. Even now, I feel tears of gratitude well up when I think of what he had done, because I knew it was his way of saying he was sorry and that he loved me and wanted me to be happy.

Because I was in charge of my trip, I took my time driving. I stopped to see sights along the way. I stayed at nice motels and sat by pools reading a book, sometimes crying behind my sunglasses with both sadness and relief.

I was a young, divorced woman with choices, and I did not know what I would do with myself when I got home. It wasn't until I pulled into the driveway and saw the wreckage of the house that I realized what I had done, and I wasn't at all happy about it.

Faye was waiting for me, sitting on the crumbling stone steps. Although she had grown up in Whispering Pines, she was younger than me, so I hadn't known her well. But she was working for dad's attorney, and since she told him she knew me, he had put her in charge of taking care of his estate for me.

Faye later told me she had asked him, pleaded with him, to let her handle the situation. She said that she just knew that I belonged back in Whispering Pines, which is why she pushed so hard for me to come home.

So, it was Faye who talked me through the plans to move and who I checked in with each night as I made my way across the country. And it was Faye who helped bring back the magic I had known, but that came much later.

So that's how I reunited with Faye. Bonnie came next.

Fifteen

"Well, that was enlightening. Or not." That was Peggy, blunt as usual.

Throwing her long braid woven with multicolored strands onto her back, Peggy stood, stretched, and wiggled her hips, making the braid swing back and forth. Watching Peggy was always a show.

"And now I'm bored, and I think we should do something else."

Seeing my face, she quickly added, "Well, not bored. But then, maybe yes, bored. I knew that story. And we've been sitting all day. Let's either go walk with your pet raven or do something more exciting."

I stifled the urge to say that Jay was not my pet and come back at her for her remark about becoming bored. But it wasn't worth it. I knew exactly what she was doing. In her own way, Peggy was still dragging me out from behind a garbage bin. The past was past. What do I want to do now?

"Well," Bonnie said, picking up her purse and her cardigan, "I'm going home. I wasn't bored, though, Mabel. I didn't know most of that story you told."

She gave Peggy a look as she said that, kissed me on the cheek, and started out the door until she remembered that Peggy had driven them all there.

"And thanks for the ride here, Peggy, but I can walk home from here. It's a beautiful day."

"Nope," Peggy said. "I'll drive you both home. I brought you here, I'll get you back."

Faye stood too. Standing next to Peggy, she could have been sitting. Peggy was a goddess, and Faye was a tiny fairy. With her shoulder-length hair now a dark gray, pulled back with a violet bow that matched her violet tunic that she wore over her yoga pants, Faye looked as if she could dance off into my garden and live with the flowers.

"Coming?" Peggy asked, looking at me.

"Where?" I asked. I was worried and had a right to be. You never knew what Peggy was up to. But at the same time, I was bored too. That realization hit me like a ton of bricks. I was bored. How could that be?

Suddenly, I felt a tingle that started at the bottom of my feet and rose like a storm up through every pore of my body. I stared at the three women in front of me as if I were seeing them for the first time. I had friends. What had I been thinking while sitting at home, waiting to fall down the stairs and break my neck?

I swear it was as if a light was switched on in the room. Everything lit up for a moment. I felt Jay's claws digging into my shoulder, which was impossible given that I was in my house. Then he pecked me on the head. The light faded, and Peggy, Bonnie, and Faye were staring at me as if I had gone crazy.

Had I?

"What's wrong with you?" Peggy asked.

Faye didn't ask. She just came over and hugged me. "Good to see you again, Mabel."

It was the exact same thing she had said to me all those years ago as I stepped out of my car. She had hugged me that day, too. She smelled like gardenias, just as she did back then. But back then, her hair was dark and shiny, and her eyes were bright and filled with something I couldn't put my finger on. They still were.

"You've seen me before?" I said, completely forgetting that I had met her when we were children.

"We've known each other for years, Mabel," she answered, and then laughed her soft laugh that sounded like water bubbling over rocks in a stream.

That day, I was too tired and distressed to tell her I had no memory of her from before, so I figured she was mistaken. I hated the way the house looked. I missed Los Angeles. I had no time for the mystery that was Faye.

Later, I understood what she meant that day. Not only had we known each other as children, but we had also known each other in other lifetimes. This was not something often discussed, but like Harry, Faye and I had known each other before.

Last time, I lied when I said, "It's good to be home." But this time I said it with feeling, and I meant it. "It's good to be home."

Peggy and Bonnie took all of this in stride. Strange things happened around Faye. And me too, but I didn't think they knew that. *The things I have kept from my friends*, I thought. *Unless I hadn't.*

Staring back at my friends, I decided that this was the beginning of a new era for me, the new Mabel. This era would be full of things that I consciously chose to do. And it started now because I was fully aware that there was only so much time left to get by.

"It's nothing," I said to Peggy as casually as possible, as if I said this kind of thing every day. "I don't care where we go. You lead the way."

Out of the corner of my eye, I saw Jay and Dove sitting on a branch of the large maple tree in my front yard. They both cocked their heads and flew away, croaking some kind of message as they went.

I took it as a sign that they agreed with what was happening.

I put the shiny phone I didn't know how to use in my purse, grabbed the new sweater I had bought when Grace and I went shopping, and followed my friends out the door. I didn't bother locking the door behind me. After all, what did I have to steal? The only thing of value in that house was the book, and it had already taken itself away.

Bonnie sat up front with Peggy as she drove, and Faye and I sat in the back seat. All I wanted to do was giggle. So I did. Over nothing. Soon everyone was giggling, and the world had become bright with promise.

Only too soon we would have things to face, people to save, and decisions to make, but on that day, on the fourth of May, in Peggy's car going nowhere in particular, we giggled because we wanted to, and it felt great.

Later, when the world darkened for a time, I remembered that day and held onto it as if it were a precious jewel, because it was. And eventually, that memory saved us all.

But first, we had a journey to take. Each one of us, in our own way, had to come to terms with who we were and choices we had made. But at least we did it together. Mostly.

Sixteen

Although our town had the lovely name of Whispering Pines, it hadn't always been a particularly beautiful town. Now it seemed a little more charming., but it could still do with some upgrades. Like me, it seemed to have decided to just get by.

As we drove through town, heading to wherever Peggy was taking us, I wondered if there was something I could do to wake it up along with me. Besides fixing up my house, maybe I could join some kind of "cleanup and beautify the town" group.

I put that idea on my mental list of ideas for something meaningful to do. I doubted that was the answer, but at least it was a start. I didn't bother asking where we were going; Peggy would take us somewhere, and I would enjoy it. That's what I told myself, and I meant it.

We didn't go far after all. Whispering Pines is a fairly small town. Some people would say it was a nothing town. It was stuck in the middle of the woods, with only small, two-lane roads leading in and out of it.

But its remoteness was why I had loved it when I was little and learned to love it again when I returned. Whispering Pines has always been a quiet, private, and peaceful town surrounded by woods filled with maple trees, pines, birds, and animals of all kinds.

I knew it used to be a logging town, but that had stopped long ago. When mom, dad, and I lived here, it was barely surviving. I never knew what Harry's parents, really his dad, did for a living in such a small town. His mom was what women were expected to be back then: a stay-at-home mom.

That's what my mom was, too. But she seemed content with it. I'm not so sure about Harry's mom. She never seemed happy, and I think she drank a lot.

My dad was a banker both when we lived in Whispering Pines and in Los Angeles. I had never put it together before that we had both worked with money. Maybe I was more like my dad than I thought.

Now Whispering Pines is billed as a place to get away from it all, and with the rise of the internet and people working from home, it has revived a bit. I had heard from Grace that a few small cottage industries had started selling local products, like the syrup that flowed from our trees and handmade crafts.

Whispering Pines had found a new way to exist in the world, and I was going to follow its example. Maybe help it along a bit while helping myself.

It had been years since I had gone anywhere other than home and the restaurant where Grace worked, so I was pleasantly surprised when Peggy parked in front of a cozy-looking diner that I had never seen before and announced, "First we eat, then we dance!"

Bonnie's face turned pale, Faye clapped her hands together, and I squeaked out, "Dance?"

"Oh, get over yourself," Peggy said to all of us as she unclipped her seat belt and bounced out of the car. "Line dancing. Lessons. Fun."

Sure, I thought as I followed her into the diner. *Fun.* But I had agreed to live again, and if this is what it took, this is what I would do.

We slid into a booth directly in front of the long counter, with round bar stools bolted to the floor in front of it. Behind the counter was an opening where I could see cooks bustling around and steam rising from the grill.

If it had been up to me, I would have chosen a booth in the back, but Peggy was having none of that. A waitress waved at her as we came in. A few people at the bar turned around and said "hi" too. Even the cooks looked up, smiled, and nodded.

Good Lord, I thought. *She knows everyone.* By the time Lucy, our waitress, had taken our order, Peggy had said hi to every single person in that diner, introduced them all and announced we were going line dancing after we ate. If I could have sunk through the floor, I would have.

But I seemed to be the only one having a problem. Both Faye and Bonnie knew some of the people in the diner. I was surprised that Faye did, but then I had no idea what she had been up to the last eleven years. I made a mental note to find out.

If I kept on making mental notes, I was going to have to start carrying around a notebook. Or learn how to use the phone. Grace had already explained to me that I could use it for notes. It made no sense to me. How could a phone take notes?

The fact that Bonnie knew most of the people didn't surprise me. She had either taught them, their kids, or grandkids. Even now, at sixty and retired, she still substitutes whenever she can. I only knew that fact because Grace told me she often saw Bonnie at her school.

I had met Bonnie when Jenny started first grade. Although Bonnie was only twenty-seven, even then she had the air of being everyone's idea of their favorite grandmother. She was warm, attentive, and deeply committed to each child.

Bonnie wasn't Jenny's teacher until later, but she went out of her way to meet the students that would soon be in her classroom. And their parents. Which meant Harry and I would see her during parent meetings at the school.

Even then, I was a hard person to get to know. It was Faye who insisted that I become friends with her, and it was Faye who rounded up Bonnie when we did things together.

But that didn't happen for years, because at first it was just Faye and me. Peggy was off doing her thing and sending post cards once in a while, and Harry was living the writer's life in Vermont. I only knew that because Faye told me. She eventually told me that she had told a little white lie about Harry visiting. I forgave her for it eventually because of what ended up happening, and because that white lie had gotten me to return home.

However, back then, still upset, I refused to read his books or learn anything about what he was doing. It was much too painful.

Instead, I threw myself into bringing the house back to life and taking walks in the woods. Sometimes with Faye. Usually by myself. Thanks to my investing and my father's money, I didn't have to work. Maybe that wasn't a good thing. Maybe for all these years, I have been too isolated.

Actually, there was no maybe about it. For eleven years, I had been waiting for Harry to come back the way he always did. I was alone in my house, with Grace and the ravens for company. Of course, I knew Harry couldn't come back this time. And as hard as I wished it would happen, I couldn't follow him wherever he went.

But all that isolation was over now. Peggy was going to make sure of that. And I had agreed, even though a huge part of me was screaming no, although all we had done so far was slide into a booth in a diner and order some food. I tried to delay leaving the restaurant for as long as I could. I pushed peas around on my plate until Faye told me to hurry up and finish. It was time for line dancing.

How could that go wrong? I wondered. I already had a plan for how to get out of it. I'd go, but I wouldn't be dancing.

Seventeen

But I was wrong. I danced. I could lie and say that I hated every minute of it, but I didn't.

Peggy had driven us just a few blocks down the street to a place that looked exactly like what a bar should look like in a small town. The parking lot was already half full, but Peggy said not to worry. This wasn't the drinking crowd, this was the dancing crowd. I didn't tell her it wasn't the drinking part that worried me.

Peggy practically danced out of the car, while Faye, Bonnie, and I followed at a slight distance. Maybe we were deciding if we wanted to be seen with this wild woman. Bonnie kept looking around at the parking lot, probably wondering if she could find someone to take her home, but Faye hooked her arm through ours and said, "Come on. It will be fun!"

As the door opened, I glimpsed a dark room, fairy lights strung along the edges of the wall, and smelled the faint whiff of smoked meat and stale beer. Once again, it felt like the entire room turned around and greeted Peggy.

Watching her wave, smile, and wiggle her way through the room, leading us to a booth along the wall, I marveled at her willingness to be seen exactly as she was. But then, she had always been this way. Maybe not quite as extravagantly. But she told me years before that when she hit sixty, and after getting divorced for the third time, she had decided not to worry about how other people saw her.

She'd feel good and hope that made others feel good, too. If they chose not to, then the heck with them. She just didn't have to hang around them. Which made me wonder how she still hung around me; I was the Debby Downer of the group. Or had been for too many years.

As soon as we sat down, the server was there, and we all ordered drinks of some kind. Peggy said they were on her because she was so delighted to have us join her in one of her favorite activities. Bonnie still looked like I felt, but Faye had lit up with excitement. It was then that I remembered how much Faye loved to dance. What else have I forgotten?

I sipped my diet soda and tried to make myself invisible. When the dance teacher came out of the back room and waved at everyone to get up, I slumped down in my seat.

While Peggy was driving us to the bar that I didn't even know existed, she explained that they gave line dancing lessons early in the evening for free as long as you bought a drink. And since line dancing didn't require a partner, it was perfect for all of us single women.

"Single women," I had said, laughing.

"Well, do you see any men here with us?" Peggy demanded, pointing around the car.

She had a point. I was single. My first husband could be dead, for all I knew. And for me, there had only ever been Harry, which is why that first marriage was a mistake. But then how was I to know that I would see Harry again?

Peggy had three husbands. One died, one she divorced, and one divorced her. The last one was why she had come to Whispering Pines, saying she needed to start life over again, and why not do it with me? But how much help had I been? Had she dated since then? I almost started crying when I realized that I didn't know.

How selfish had I been? Another mental note was made. I ticked them off with my fingers. Fix the house, help fix the town, and find out if Peggy has been dating. I switched the last one to find out if any of my friends have been dating.

Or at least find out what they have been doing for the last eleven years. Who cared about the dating? What I wanted to know was, were they happy?

And for God's sake, I said to myself, *fix yourself up*. That last mental note was added when I looked around the room filled with people getting ready to dance, and I saw all the other women and some men, all looking spiffy and dressed up. On the other hand, I was wearing clothes I had had forever. Except for my new sweater.

"Let's go," Peggy said, and everyone did as she said except me.

Peggy glared. I said I had a bad back.

"You're a terrible liar," she said, pulling me up onto the dance floor.

Within minutes, all of my mental notes and worries went out of my head as we followed the instructor. I cursed under my breath as I tried to follow her instructions. Clap here, kick there, turn around, and turn around again.

It was confusing at first, and then it wasn't. Then it was just plain fun, and I started laughing out loud.

For the next hour, life was a joy. And I wondered once again why I had tuned it out. Then I realized I hadn't glimpsed Harry all day and realized that was one reason I hadn't let myself have fun. I was afraid I'd lose him all together if I did. I had been telling myself that a wisp of a ghost was better than nothing.

As I stomped, clapped, and twirled, I realized that was a lie. Wherever Harry was, he would wait for me. But he would never have wanted me to stop living.

I had wasted eleven good years of what was, in retrospect, a very short life. I looked over at Peggy and she winked at me and then tilted her head towards Bonnie.

I looked and gasped out loud, but the music was too loud for anyone to hear me. Bonnie was standing on the sidelines, pretending to be watching all the dancers, but she was actually looking at a man in a cowboy shirt as if she were a teenager in love.

"Who is that?" I hissed at Peggy.

She shrugged, "Don't know. But I intend to find out."

Eighteen

Although the line dance lesson lasted only an hour, I was thoroughly exhausted by the time we had danced the last dance, everyone cheering and stomping their feet and smiling at each other as if they had known each other forever.

Returning to our booth, I panted a little, hoping no one noticed. Then I realized everyone was out of breath and stopped worrying about it. Instead, I directed my attention to Bonnie, who had slid in across from me. Her face was flushed even though she hadn't been dancing as much as we were, so I had to assume that it was because of that man.

Having decided to stop hiding and hyped up from the dancing, I didn't beat around the bush. "Who was that guy you were staring at?"

Peggy snorted. Faye smiled. Bonnie blanched. I waited.

"Okay, yes, I was staring at him. I don't know who he is. All I know is that his name is Jack. I've seen him around town, but that's it."

Given that Bonnie had never married and rarely dated, it really wasn't just "that's it," but we gave her a break and let it be. If I was going to return to the land of the living, I was also determined to make sure my friends were happy. So I bit back my retort, "Isn't he a little young for you?" and let it be. For now.

Sitting in the booth, amidst the laughter and the soft, warm glow of the fairy lights, I was content for the first time in years. The day spent with my friends reminded me that life is short, and clinging to the past, to the ghosts of what might have been, only steals away the present. Harry, my long-lost love, would have wanted me to live fully, not just linger in the shadows of his memory.

Peggy drove us all home, dropping me off last. She got out of the car and walked me to the house, hugging me at the front door. It felt the same as when she first rescued me. I hugged her back, thanked her for everything, and turned to go into the house before I broke down in tears again.

I didn't know how much I missed my friends and a life filled with things to do until Peggy dragged me back into life. I had so many things to talk to Grace about.

I fell asleep not with a yearning for Harry but with a heart full of gratitude for the here and now and a spark of excitement for what tomorrow might bring. For the first time in what felt like forever, I was actually looking forward to the new day.

The next morning, I woke up to the smell of coffee. I thought I was dreaming. Harry used to make me coffee every morning and bring it to me in bed. But when I opened my eyes, it was Grace smiling at me as she put a mug of coffee on the nightstand.

Then she pulled a chair up, propped her feet up on my bed, and said, "Spill it, Gammy. What have you been up to?"

"Why am I still in bed? Why are you here?"

"It's morning. The sun is up. And I know you are still in bed because you were gallivanting all over town last night!"

Grace reached over and stacked pillows behind me as I struggled to sit up, trying to make sense of the light spilling into the bedroom, coffee by the bed, and Grace smiling at me. It reminded me of when she was little and Harry was still alive. She was sometimes allowed to stay overnight with us, and in the morning she would snuggle between us.

A pang of sadness for what was gone ran through me, and I had to struggle to keep from crying. I covered it up with a curse. Picking up my coffee, I sipped it, knowing Grace would have made it just the way I liked it. I was trying to decide what to say next.

"I wouldn't say we were gallivanting all over town. Besides, who told you?"

Grace held up her phone, showing me a screen with lots of words on it. It meant nothing to me.

"Emails, texts, even a phone call or two. Everyone is telling me they saw you out dancing."

"Everyone? Why would they care? Who's everyone anyway?"

"Okay, not everyone. But there are lots of people. And because they were happy to see you. You've been missing for a while."

I couldn't wrap my head around the fact that enough people knew me, noticed me, and told my granddaughter because they knew I had been missing. How had they noticed? Why had they noticed? Who had I been before that so many people knew me?

Grace must have known what I was thinking, and reached over to hold my hand. "Gammy, don't you know?"

I stared at her, shaking my head, not understanding.

"Yes, everyone loved Granddad, but it was you who brought peace to people's lives. Lots of people."

I thought Grace had gone mad. Or I had. Maybe I had died, and this was another lifetime. *Not impossible*, I thought. *But probably not.*

However, last night everyone smiled and said "hi" to my friends, but not to me. Or had I not noticed, thinking that I was still invisible? *No*, I decided. *Grace had it all wrong. No one in town knew me, let alone missed me.*

Grace gave me a look. She reminded me of Peggy.

"Get up. Get dressed. First, you are going to learn how to use your phone, and then we are going shopping. Along the way, perhaps your memory of who you are will return. If not. I'm calling in the cavalry."

By that, I knew she meant Peggy, Bonnie, and Faye. And then I realized that all of what she said sounded fun.

Maybe I had died, and this was a new me. If so, I was going to enjoy every minute or die trying. With that thought, I started to giggle. Die trying. Funny. It's much different from thinking about falling down the stairs and breaking my neck.

Yes, things were moving along just fine. Besides, I needed to find out who that man Jack was and see if he was right for Bonnie.

With my morning routine down pat, I was ready to go within fifteen minutes. I didn't know about the phone thing. It seemed like it was going to be hard, but I was determined to learn.

An hour later, it was Grace who was cursing as she tried to get me to understand how it worked. But at least I could make and receive phone calls, and I even answered a text from Grace.

We both considered that enough progress for the day and headed off to breakfast and shopping.

Neither one of us knew what we were going to find, but then, wasn't that what life was about? It was a treasure hunt. I was ready. Or so I thought.

Nineteen

Breakfast was a lively affair, with Grace chattering about the latest happenings in town and me listening, still trying to piece together this newfound awareness of the appreciation people seemed to have for me.

This time I noticed people said "hi," not just to Grace but to me too. Still not understanding, I nodded and smiled back. Grace patted me on the back like I was a little kid and told me she was proud of me. When had this role reversal taken place, anyway?

After breakfast, we hit the stores. Shopping with Grace was an experience in itself. She had a keen eye for fashion and insisted I try on things I would never have picked for myself. To my surprise, I enjoyed the process, laughing at some of the outrageous choices, and feeling a sense of renewal with each new outfit I tried on.

As we moved from store to store, I noticed more people wave and smile at me. Some even stopped to chat, expressing their joy at seeing me out and about. It was overwhelming and heartwarming at the same time. It seemed Grace was right—people remembered me, and more importantly, they cared.

I was afraid to tell Grace that I couldn't remember most of the people or understand why they were happy to see me. At first, I thought maybe it was the first sign of Alzheimer's, but then I remembered it was the other way around. People with Alzheimer's remember the past but can't remember the present.

For some reason, I had blocked out a huge chunk of my life. The part where I knew many people and made them happy.

Amidst the flurry of shopping, my phone buzzed with a text message. Fumbling with the device, I managed to open it—it was from Peggy, inviting us to join her, Bonnie, and Faye for lunch. Grace beamed at the invitation, and we quickly agreed to meet them.

Lunch was a riot. The table was alive with laughter, stories, and shared memories. Peggy tried to convince Bonnie to tell us about Jack. She refused, saying it was nothing and just let it go. Faye took the attention off of Bonnie by talking about how much she had liked the line dance class. And Peggy, as always, was the life of the party, regaling us with tales of her latest adventures.

As we all talked and laughed, I felt a profound sense of belonging. Even though I had realized that I couldn't remember a huge chunk of my life, these women, my friends, were a testament to the life I had lived. And it seemed that it had been one that was full of love, laughter, and now, new beginnings.

As the afternoon waned, I realized that this was more than just a day out. It was a turning point, a reawakening of sorts. Grace was right. It was time to relearn who I was—whoever that was—and to embrace the life that was waiting for me.

The day ended with promises to meet again soon. As Grace and I headed home, I felt a renewed sense of purpose. Yes, it was time to live again, not just for Harry or for my granddaughter, but for myself.

That night, as I lay in bed, I didn't feel the usual pang of loneliness. Instead, I felt a quiet anticipation of what the future might hold. Whispering Pines wasn't just a place where I existed. It was a community where I belonged, and I was ready to rediscover my place in it.

However, as lovely as the last two days had been, I was worried. Why would I forget my place in the community? I could understand why the last eleven years were a blur. I made them that way. I stayed in by myself, only venturing out to go for a walk with Jay. Ignoring the neighbors so they wouldn't talk to me. I remembered all that because there wasn't much to remember.

But before that, what could I remember? Why had I forgotten? Was that why the book of memories existed—to remind me of what I had forgotten? But then, this year, it didn't show up. Why? Based on the last few days, I had to think that it was because I was supposed to remember all of it on my own.

All I had were questions and no proper answers. I had started to tell Grace the story of my life. I remembered it clearly up until... well, that was the thing. Up until when?

Before I fell asleep, I reached over and grabbed the shiny phone, and remembering what Grace had taught me, I texted her and asked if she would come over again in the morning.

The words "of course" popped up within seconds, accompanied by a large red heart. She'd have to show me how to do that, too. *No wonder people liked these things, I thought. Instant communication.* As I said those words to myself, a flash of memory went by, but then it was gone.

But that flash encouraged me. I hadn't lost my memories; they were buried in there somewhere, and I was going to dig them up. Quelling the fear that rose in me, I reminded myself of my promise to Grace and my friends to come back to the land of the living before I left it for good.

Breathing in and out, listening to my breath, and blocking everything else out of my mind, I fell asleep. But just before I did, the smell of lilacs drifted past me. I didn't have time to wonder why before sleep took me away.

Twenty

"Okay," Grace said. We had just finished our daily coffee and pastries that she had brought with her. "Let's start with when you moved back here. What did you do after you moved back to Whispering Pines?"

I smiled, thinking that this part might be easy. Returning to Whispering Pines was something that I remembered. I remembered Faye and the smell of gardenias as she hugged me at the door that first day. I remembered walking into an absolutely filthy house filled with memories.

Seeing the house for the first time in fourteen years had been a shock. I had left as a child at ten and returned as a young, worldly woman at twenty-four. At twenty-four, I thought I was a grown-up. Now I see everyone under forty as a child.

But that day, I didn't know that. I thought I could handle anything. But staring at the neglected house, I doubted myself. I wasn't even sure I could stand to be in the house for even one night. But I didn't have a choice. Although Faye had told me I could stay at her house, being stubborn, I had refused. So Faye had hugged me and then driven away.

Trying not to breathe too deeply in that musty house, I put my suitcase down and checked my watch. I had eighteen hours until Faye would return and take me to see Dad's attorney and then to go buy a car. But until then, with no way to reach her, I was stuck.

That first night in the house, I barely slept. Thanks to Faye, there was food in the fridge and a cot with blankets in the living room, but the otherwise empty house felt alive. It was the first time since I was ten that I thought I saw people who weren't there.

Across the street, Harry's old house looked even worse than mine did, and of course there was no longer the comfort in knowing that my best friend was living there. He wasn't, and I knew he never would again.

I lay on that hard cot, the soft blankets Faye had brought wrapped around me. I cried for everything I had lost. All I could think about was that my life was shattered. I had no family. And I was back to being crazy.

Although, as a child, I enjoyed my visions of people and things that weren't really there, alone in an old house, now I was terrified. I decided to fix up the house enough to sell and leave Whispering Pines altogether. The sooner, the better.

"But you didn't leave, even though the house was a mess." Grace broke into my thoughts.

I sighed and decided not to tell Grace about the visions, since that seemed too weird, so I simply said, "No, I didn't."

"Why did you stay?"

Closing my eyes, I returned to that time. Why hadn't I left? I knew I wanted to. But I also knew I couldn't go back to my old life in Los Angeles. I had cut all my ties, so I dreamed about moving somewhere new. Maybe not even in America.

It was a lovely dream, one that kept me going for a long time as I fixed up the house in order to sell it. Even now, I could feel the yearning that I had to live somewhere else. But it was as if the house roped me in and wouldn't let me go.

I knew I couldn't sell the house until all the repairs were done, and that took much longer than I thought it would. By then, I had settled into a routine, and things were looking better in Whispering Pines.

A young couple had bought the house across the street and was fixing it up before their first child arrived. We shared handymen and notes about our houses. As we improved our homes, other people did too, and the street slowly returned to the beautiful neighborhood I had known as a child.

I stopped for a minute before trying to decide how much to tell Grace about the things I saw in the woods and in the house. I thought that perhaps I had blocked out a part of my life because of those visions. What had I seen and when?

As I paused to think about what to tell Grace next, a phone rang. I didn't realize what it was until Grace pointed to the phone on the table beside me. Then I remembered Grace had somehow programmed my phone, so there was a distinct ring for each friend. This was Peggy.

Grace reminded me how to answer it, and Peggy said loud enough for Grace to hear, "I want to come over to talk about something."

"What?" I asked and then wondered if I was always this blunt and abrupt with people.

Probably often, because Peggy didn't skip a beat as if she were used to it. She just said she'd be there in a few and hung up.

As Grace got up to go, I asked her to stay. I had nothing to hide, at least not something I could remember, except maybe the visions, and Peggy never cared about hiding anything. At least that I knew of, or, as I reminded myself, remembered.

Who knew what was buried in my memories? For a second, I thought of a shovel digging something, and then it was gone. I had planted something. *Well, of course I did*, I thought. *I was always planting something.*

The back door that led out to the garden was open, so there was just the screen door between me and the outside. It was my favorite time of year, and I didn't want to miss a moment of it.

But as I remembered the digging, the smell of lilacs drifted through. I thought I had imagined it, but Grace smiled and said, "That's one of my favorite smells."

"What?"

Grace laughed and said, "The lilacs, of course. You must smell it. It's one of your favorite smells, too."

While she was talking, Grace walked to the back door and leaned out, "Yep, the lilac bush has bloomed."

"What lilac bush?" I asked before I could stop myself.

When Grace turned to me with an anxious face, I added, "Oh, you mean that one?"

But I didn't know what lilac bush she meant. I joined her at the back door and saw an enormous lilac beside the stairs, and wondered how long that had been there.

As if she were reading my mind, Grace said, "Remember, you and granddad planted it a few years before he died."

I smiled as I said, "Of course I remember." But I didn't.

Twenty One

When Peggy arrived, she brought a whirlwind with her. As she stepped out of the car, her long hair flew around her head, caught up in a wind that had just arrived. Flower petals swirled in the air and then settled back down again.

I only had a moment to notice that the colors in Peggy's hair matched the flower petals because I blinked, and when I opened my eyes, the wind was gone, and Peggy's hair was pulled back into a ponytail, and there weren't any flower petals on the ground.

Yes, I thought *I had gone crazy.* Once again, a memory swept through, one that I couldn't hold on to, but it was enough to remind me that this kind of thing had happened before. I didn't understand it, so I kept quiet about it. Did anyone want to admit when they were losing their mind?

But then, based on what I was beginning to remember about the visions I used to have, I might have been losing my mind my whole life. And if that was so, maybe it was who I really was. Still, I wasn't ready to talk about it.

Ushering Peggy into the house, I directed her to her favorite chair and went into the kitchen to get her a cup of coffee. One cream, no sugar. Years of habit kicked in as I settled myself down. It was nothing I told myself; all of what was happening and remembering was just an overactive imagination. That's all it's ever been.

Peggy accepted the coffee, took a sip, smiled at me, leaned forward, and whispered, "I'm worried about Bonnie."

"Why are you whispering? She's not here," I said.

Peggy laughed, pulled the scrunchie out of her hair, and let her hair fall down her back. "Creating drama? But seriously, I am worried. She seems to have fallen for that Jack."

"And?"

"And I don't think he is what he appears to be."

A piercing pain went through my head, right between my eyes, as if someone had stabbed me with a sharp object. I reached up, but nothing was there.

"See, you feel it too."

Seeing my puzzled face, she added, "That pain you just got."

I stared at Peggy. *How did she know? Had this happened before?* Maybe it was time to tell Grace and Peggy what I was starting to remember about myself. The crazy visions. Because, as much as I tried to deny it, I was going to need help.

"What? You think I don't know? Everyone knows. That's why everyone is so happy to have you moving around the world again."

I gathered my courage and asked, "Know what?"

Peggy stood up and stared down at me, slumped in my chair.

"What kind of game are you playing, Mabel? We all gave you eleven years to get yourself back together. For eleven years, we waited for you to return to the land of the living.

"Do you think it was easy for us? Not only did we miss you, you little twerp, but we needed your help, and you weren't there. And now you're still hiding? What will it take, Mabel, to get you to stop feeling sorry for yourself?"

Grace stood too, faced Peggy, and said, "Don't talk to my grandmother that way!"

I started giggling. They both looked at me, and Peggy, keeping her stern face on, demanded, "What's so funny?"

"Twerp?"

It took only a second longer until the two of them were giggling along with me. Every time one of us would stop, the other would say, "twerp?" and that would start us off again.

Finally, the giggling stopped, with none of us really understanding why we had laughed so hard at that word. Maybe it was the combination of how mad Peggy was along with a word I hadn't heard used since I was a kid, but somehow it short-circuited my brain, and I could see the humor in my problem.

"The truth is, Peggy, I don't remember."

"Remember what?"

"What I used to do before Harry died. I was completely shocked to realize that not only did people in Whispering Pines know me, but they seemed to like me. I remember moving here and other big events, but not the day-to-day stuff.

"So when you say I used to help people, and I have gotten that pain before, I don't have a clue what you mean. Maybe that part of me, the part you are referring to, died when Harry died."

As Peggy stared at me, her glare turning to confusion and a touch of pity, I realized that what I said couldn't be true. If that part of me had died with Harry, then how could I explain the weird things that had been happening the last few days.

Peggy realized that at the same time as I did.

"If that were true, why did you get the same pain as you used to get when you saw something. What did you see?"

Shaking my head, I said, "I got the pain. I didn't see anything. Is that what is supposed to happen? I see things?"

"Yes, you saw things, but you also knew things. So do you know something about Jack?"

Pausing for a moment, I didn't think I did. "Are you saying I am some kind of witch or psychic?"

"No. You said that was an erroneous term. Instead, you told us that there are people who have a gift for observation and awareness, and that awareness provides them with information. You said everyone has the innate ability, but most people don't notice it or allow it.

"But you nurtured your gift, and that gave you insights into people and things. You saw things that the rest of us missed. You often talked about the beauty of our interconnection within the infinite."

"Oh. Hum. Sounds lovely or scary. Which one was it?"

"I never asked you before. I guess both; otherwise, why have you forgotten? But we need you to get back in touch with that part of yourself. It's not gone; you just went into hiding. That's what I think, anyway."

Flipping her hair back and sitting up straighter in her chair, she leaned forward as she said, "It's time to come out from behind the dumpster where you put your own self this time."

I got the reference. She was right about me being behind the dumpster, but I wondered why I had put myself there. Was it like the first time? Was I afraid? Of what?

All along, I had thought it was grief that had kept me locked away in my house. Maybe it was more than that.

Grace had watched the two of us without saying anything. When we both went quiet, she spoke up.

"I remember magic days with you, Gammy. I know you think it was just Granddad I came over to see when I was a little girl. But you knew things.

"But then granddad died, and mom wasn't happy about me coming to see you without him here. But I missed our time together and finally convinced her. However, the magic part of you was missing.

"The last few days, though, I felt it again. Don't you?"

Looking at the two of them, I let myself drift back in time and caught a glimpse of what they were saying. Then it was gone.

"Yes. A tiny bit. So if you both are willing to help me, I want to remember. And help Bonnie if she is in trouble."

"Why not keep going with the story?" Grace said. "You remembered moving into this house. Who were you then? Why did you stay? When did Harry come back?"

Twenty Two

"Can we talk over lunch?" I asked. "I'm not stalling. I'm just hungry."

When Peggy and Grace both gave me the same look, I added. "Okay, I'm stalling a little, but really, I'm hungry."

Within a few minutes, we had decided to order in, and Grace called her favorite restaurant, another one I didn't remember, and asked them to deliver.

While we waited, I took myself back to the years of rebuilding the house.

This time I told them about the visions I had seen the first night. At the time, I had written it off as stress from all the changes I had made and all the memories I had buried inside myself about living there as a child.

That night, my memories were so intense that I could hear my mother and father's laughter as they worked together on the weekends in the kitchen.

"They actually cooked and made up recipes together," I shared.

"What did they make?" Grace asked. She hadn't known her great-grandparents, so I told her stories about them while we waited for lunch to arrive.

"They were always together. As soon as dad came home from work, mom would join him for a walk around the garden. They were each other's best friends.

"No wonder he was devastated when she died," Peggy said. "Do you still see them?"

I thought back and realized that I hadn't seen them since that first night. Perhaps they were only waiting for me to come home before they left together for good.

When I shared that insight, both Grace and Peggy agreed, and then lunch arrived, and we moved off that subject. But I knew that I was right. They had waited for me to come home.

Which, of course, made me think of Harry. I had never put those two things together before. I saw Harry but didn't think anything of it, maybe just putting the visions into the category that everyone saw their loved ones after they died.

But I knew they didn't. I hadn't forgotten everything. So what had I forgotten?

"What kind of vision and knowing did I used to have? How did I help people?"

I asked that question just as both Grace and Peggy were in the process of slurping up noodles from the soup we ordered. Peggy eyed me as the last of the noodles disappeared into her mouth and held up a finger as she chewed them before answering. "Nope. Not getting out of it that easily. You'll remember. Keep talking."

So I continued where I had left off. The first years back at Whispering Pines flew by. I was busy fixing the house and walking in the woods. I joined the gardening club but discovered that they were more into domesticated plants, and I loved the wildness of the woods. I had a little garden in the back where I grew vegetables, but other than that, things grew wild in my yard.

When Faye came over to visit, she walked the woods with me too. She knew so much more about each plant and tree than I did. I loved the feeling of being in nature and often pretended that I was a tree, plant, or bird so I could imagine what life was like for them.

Faye moved through the woods the same way Harry did. In many ways, they were the same. I could only think of one word to describe them: elusive. Yet ever-present at the same time. It was as if they lived in a different version of reality than the rest of us.

"Did you date?" Grace asked.

"No. I had decided that I didn't need anyone. I liked being single and doing what I felt like doing. I joined groups in town, then got bored and quit them. I kept myself busy keeping up the house and reading."

"And then Harry came back," Peggy asked.

"Not really. Not then. At least that was not his intention. He was on a book tour and thought he'd stop by Whispering Pines and see his old house. His plan was to take a walk in the woods that he grew up in and get more stories for his books. He was going to visit for a few days and then never come back."

There was a tap at the kitchen window. Looking up, we all saw Jay waiting for me. Then Dove joined him, and they both cocked their heads at the three of us. It was clear to me what they wanted.

And they were right; it was a beautiful day outside. It was time to go for a walk. Grace had walked with me and the ravens before, but Peggy never had. She couldn't stop staring at the two of them as they led the way to the lake.

As we walked, I realized that my neighbors had been watching me do this for years, and yet I had barely acknowledged them. It amazed me that they were still willing to wave back when I waved more enthusiastically at them this time.

Of course, it was all easier because of Peggy, because besides staring at Jay and Dove, she made sure she said hi to everyone who was outside enjoying the beautiful spring day.

Once we reached the lake, we sat on one of the benches, and I continued the story about Harry coming home.

I had seen him before he saw me. But it had been twenty years since I had last seen him, so I didn't know who he was. The man looking up at a tree didn't resemble the sixteen-year-old boy that I had left behind twenty years before.

I was startled at seeing a man in the woods that I didn't know, but I wasn't afraid. He felt familiar. So I said "hello," and he turned.

For a moment, we stared at each other. I suppose I should have recognized him from his picture on the back of the book that I had seen. But at the time, I had only glanced at it and never looked at it again. It hurt my heart too much to see him and know we would never be together again.

So, it was Harry who figured it out. I don't know how. I was ten when he last saw me. Then I was a grown woman. Later, he told me it was my hair and then my eyes that gave me away. Besides, I was still not much taller than when he had last seen me.

When he said my name, I knew who he was. All the years that I had dreamed of seeing him again, and there he was in front of me. I couldn't move. I didn't realize that tears were streaming down my face until one splashed on my hands.

We spent the next few days together, and then he had to go.

"But he came back," Grace said.

"He did," I answered, knowing there was much more to the story than that. Because although he was always leaving, he always came back. Except for the last time.

Twenty Three

I heard a tinkling sound coming from Peggy's direction and thought, 'What on earth is that?' and then realized it was her phone. I had left mine at home, forgetting that I should be bringing it with me all the time.

Grace had told me that's what was so wonderful about having cell phones. They were always there to support you. But I didn't believe her, thinking that was ridiculous. How could a phone support me?

Later, she showed me that she had put some apps on both our phones so I could see where she was and she could see where I was. At first, I was insulted. Then I realized I loved seeing where Grace was, especially since I knew that she would be living far from me in just a few short months.

To my surprise, I also realized that I liked that she knew where I was at all times. It felt that I could easily reach out to her, being able to see in my mind's eye where she was.

"Gotta go," Peggy said, standing up. "Some kind of emergency at the library."

Peggy volunteered all over town, so the fact that the library had called her to help with something wasn't surprising. After moving to Whispering Pines, it only took Peggy a few weeks to build a new life. She said it helped her get over feeling sorry for herself.

"But I still need to talk about Bonnie and that Jack guy. In the meantime, why not do your thing?"

"What thing?"

Peggy and Grace looked at each other.

"What?" I demanded.

Grace took my hand and helped me up from the bench—then, tucking her hand into my arm as we started walking, she said, "It's okay, Gammy. You'll remember."

An hour later, after they both had gone, I made myself a cup of tea and stepped outside to my garden. It wasn't much of a garden. I hadn't touched the vegetable garden since Harry died, so now the entire backyard was wild.

The tiny table and chair that sat on a small patio covered by a pergola that Harry had built for me was filthy, but I had brought a towel with me, knowing that it would be. After cleaning it the best that I could, I sat down. The patio stones beneath my feet were cool, which in the summer felt good. Ignoring my feet, I closed my eyes and waited. Was something supposed to happen?

At first, nothing did. Then, as I breathed in the garden, the scent of the lilac bush blew past my face, and I felt as if a door was opening. It was like seeing another place that had existed all along.

I stood in the doorway of that other place for a long time. I knew I was still in my garden, still in my body, still in my current life, but on the other side of the doorway was a whole other realm of information. And I realized it had been there all along.

It wasn't as if I was going somewhere to see this other place; I just had to open myself to see it.

I heard laughter and opened my eyes to see my mother and father and a little girl who I knew was me running through the garden.

We were playing hide-and-seek. And I remembered that day. I had looked around me, thinking someone was watching. Now I knew it had been me.

When the three of them faded away, it was just me and the garden, and it was getting cooler, so I grabbed my now-cold tea and headed back inside. Everything around me was back to normal, except now I remembered that there was much more going on than appeared on the surface.

I asked myself if I was afraid, and I realized I wasn't. If anything, I was mad at myself for missing the last eleven years of my life. Why had I forgotten that time and space are fluid? I knew it had to do with Harry's leaving, but I decided it didn't matter if I knew why. I'd figure it out sooner or later.

What I needed to do was see if Peggy was right and if something was up with that Jack guy. Since I got nothing from what I remembered Harry calling my "spidey senses," I thought it was time to use technology instead.

Yes, I had resisted the phone. But I hadn't completely resisted technology. Harry had insisted I learn how to use a computer, and I had one even though it was old and unused.

I tracked it down. It was buried beneath some sheets in the linen closet. I turned it on, and thankfully, it actually came on. We had internet services before, and I was grateful to myself for forgetting to turn them off. However, now that I had seen the instant responses from my phone, I found myself upset with how slowly the computer worked.

I took out my phone and texted Grace. "I need a new computer. Could we get one tomorrow?" I would have asked to get it right at that minute, but I knew Grace was at work.

However, she answered me almost immediately with a thumbs up and the message she'd be over in the morning. Then she added a smiley face.

Pleased with myself for taking forward steps into life, I grabbed a book, some left-over croissants, and headed up to bed. No one would care that I'd get crumbs in the bed. I'd read and eat, fall asleep, and as Shakespeare said in Hamlet, "Perchance to dream."

In the morning, I would focus on helping Bonnie. I was tired of moping. Tired of living a one-dimensional life. Books took me out of this world, and now that I remembered that I could do that without a book, I was looking forward to discovering what the last few years of my life would bring.

After my bathroom rituals and laying out my new clothes for the morning, not under the covers this time because it was warm enough to put them on the chair, I balanced the book and a plate of food on my belly and moved into another world.

I never felt the plate or the book slide off to the floor. I was too busy dreaming.

Twenty Four

In the morning, I didn't remember my dreams. I just knew I had them. All I kept with me was a sense that things were different and I had work to do. But first, I had to catch up with the rest of the world.

So when Grace picked me up, I told her that while we were out getting a computer, I wanted to get my hair cut and styled. To Grace's credit, she didn't ask why. She just smiled and said, "Oh, goody. What a fun day this will be."

I looked over at my beautiful granddaughter, who seemed to take every new thing that life and I threw at her in stride At eighteen, she was a grownup with a childlike view of the world. She was capable and thoughtful. She was always willing and helpful but did it all without draining herself.

If I believed in such things, I would have thought that Grace was sent to me to make sure I would be okay. She was like my fairy godmother.

Why wouldn't it be true that she was sent to me, I asked myself. *Maybe that is the way the world works.*

Today I wasn't sure about the magic part of my life because whatever I had experienced yesterday was out of reach today. But it didn't matter. Maybe the magic was that I had Grace, Faye, Bonnie, and Peggy by my side.

I would have loved to add my daughter Jenny to that list, but she had stopped liking me, if she ever had. I knew I had failed her, but I didn't know how. And as often as I had tried to fix it, I only made it worse. I had resigned myself to accepting it, but that didn't mean I liked it.

The morning flew by. Grace set up my new computer and spent time with me, showing me how to use it because it was a whole new world from my old one. She promised to show me more every time she came over.

After buying the computer, where I tried not to drive the salesman crazy with my questions and mostly silent curses, we went to Grace's hairdresser. While she got her hair trimmed, I got mine cut, so it was no longer stringy. Instead, it looked like it did when I was young, except it was gray instead of blond.

With new clothes, new hair, a new phone, and a new computer, I was a different woman. I never thought I would be grateful for the memory book not showing up, but I was.

After Grace dropped me off at home, promising to show me more about the computer later, I napped and then decided to walk in the woods instead of the easy trip of going to the lake and sitting.

All I had to do was decide which woods to go to. Although the house across the street had been sold again and the woods behind it had been made smaller as developments encroached upon it from the other side, it was still there.

Actually, I could also reach the same woods from the lake because the woods circled around behind the houses until they got to the lake and surrounded it with a mass of evergreens. I wondered if that's where the name of the town came from, because the rustle of all those pine needles often sounded like a whisper.

The other choice was simply going out the back door and into the woods behind our house. It was only a few acres, but Harry had made paths in it for me when he was alive. I wondered if the paths were still there. I made another mental note to find someone who could help me clear the garden and open up the paths.

Then, remembering that my mental notes kept drifting out of my head, I pulled a tablet from the drawer of the side table beside my chair and wrote them down.

- Do something to help the town.

- Clean up my garden.

- Clear the paths in the woods.

- Talk to people.

- Help Bonnie.

I stared at the list and added: Find out more about Faye, Bonnie, and Peggy's lives.

I didn't have to get new clothes, a phone, a computer, or cut my hair. I had already done that, but I wrote them on the list anyway so I could cross them off. Doing that brought a frisson of pleasure. How had I forgotten that I like doing things?

So many things had slipped away that day after Harry died. How did I let that happen?

Jay tapped on the window, reminding me to get outside. As I grabbed my new sweater and slipped on my walking shoes, I decided to go to the lake first and then into the woods from there. I wondered what Jay would think when he saw me do that. Would he come with me? Would he tell Dove about it?

Not for the first time, I wished I could understand the sounds that birds made. Instead, I imagined what they were saying. But I thought it would be the most glorious thing ever to actually speak to them.

As I prepared to go out the door, I added one more thing to my list.

- Fix the bird feeders and get bird food.

Jay jumped up as I wrote that and squawked. I pretended that he had read what I had written and approved it.

We didn't go far into the woods. I wasn't used to it yet. But we went far enough so that all I could see was the greening of the trees and the blooming of the daffodils scattered in the woods. I figured squirrels must have planted them there, having dug them up from someone's yard. Just for fun, I suppose, since they didn't eat them.

I watched a group of squirrels leap from branch to branch in the trees and admired their ability to work and play at the same time. I also knew that squirrels were relentless when they wanted something, so I decided to be more like squirrels in the future. Or maybe I always was.

Jay squawked at the squirrels, and they squawked back at him. "What are you saying?" I asked them. Oh, how I wish I could speak raven and squirrel languages.

When we returned, I was tired and hungry and wondered if I should eat or nap. The question was decided for me when my phone pinged, and Bonnie was wondering what I was up to. Would I like to go out for food?

Yes! I texted back and added a heart emoji. Grace had shown me how to respond that way, and I thought it was delightful to have so many choices of ways to express myself. However, Grace explained to me that some emojis had different meanings than I thought and advised me to stick with the hearts for now. So I did. For now.

Since Bonnie said she'd pick me up in thirty minutes, I only had time to change my clothes because the other ones had gotten dirty in the woods and brush my hair. It had been years since I had worn makeup, and I saw no reason to start again, so I was ready and waiting when she arrived.

Bonnie waved, and I waved back. Bonnie looked so happy, so I couldn't figure out why there seemed to be a dark cloud around her. Then it vanished, and I decided that I had imagined it.

Twenty Five

"Look at you!" Bonnie exclaimed as I got into the car. "You look... rejuvenated!" There was genuine admiration in her eyes, but also something else, something I couldn't quite place. Did it have anything to do with the dark cloud I had seen?

We filled the drive to the restaurant with casual chatter. Bonnie talked about her day and her plans, but never mentioned Jack. Why would she? She had never mentioned men before.

It surprised me that Bonnie was so busy. I knew she was still substituting as a teacher. I couldn't imagine her ever giving up the chance to teach. But I didn't know how busy she was in the community volunteering, just like Peggy. In fact, they volunteered on some of the same committees, and they were both part of a book group.

"A book group?" I asked. I didn't know Bonnie and Peggy were readers. How could I not know that? But I was happy that they were.

Grace had mentioned to me that the average person reads less than two books a year. It had shocked me to the core. I thought everyone read all the time. How could they not? Grace had smiled and said that over the years, TV and video games had decreased the number of books people read.

I still couldn't process that. Although I didn't really know much about video games, I watched TV. I couldn't understand how that would prevent me from burying myself in a good book every chance I got. I didn't have time to ask Bonnie what books they read, because once we pulled up to the restaurant, she was all about getting us in and seated.

We chose a cozy corner booth, and as we settled in, Bonnie asked me about my hair, which meant I had to tell her about my decision to be present in life again. I told her about my new computer and my new clothes, and she smiled at me and patted my hand, saying she was so happy to have me back

The only part I left out was that I was having visions. I wasn't sure if this was something I had ever talked about before. And if not, she might think I was losing my mind. Which was still a possibility.

As we talked, I realized how much I missed my friends and was glad they were back in my life. Well, they hadn't left my life, but now I was letting them back into my life.

Each one of them was so different. Peggy was the woman who forced us all to live out loud. Faye was the gentle wind reminding us all that life was good. And Bonnie was the steady ground under our feet. As far as I knew or remembered, there had never been any drama in Bonnie's life. Did that mean there hadn't been any fun either?

It bothered me how little I knew about my friend. Had I forgotten, or did I never know? Did we ever talk about serious things, or had we always circled around them? But Peggy's worry fueled my curiosity and concern, and finally I just blurted out, "So what's up with that guy, Jack?"

Bonnie paused, a forkful of salad halfway to her mouth, and stared at me.

"What do you mean?"

I mentally slapped myself. Had I always been that blunt? But now that I had asked, I didn't want to back down.

"Peggy told me that was the name of the guy you were staring at at the line dancing class."

Bonnie put her fork down and gave me the look that I had seen her use many times before on students who had done or said the wrong thing. Like everyone else who got that look, I trembled in my chair, wishing I had just kept my mouth shut.

A long moment passed, the look faded, and tears appeared in Bonnie's brown eyes.

"Was it that obvious?" Bonnie finally said.

I nodded, adding, "But only because it seemed so unlike you."

Bonnie dropped her head and stared at her plate, while I worried if I had ruined our friendship forever. I needed Bonnie in my life. I called myself an idiot at least three times before Bonnie raised her head and said, "It's not what you think."

I didn't get the chance to ask her what she meant because a bevy of four high school girls entered the restaurant and, seeing Bonnie, rushed over to talk to her. It turned out they were the committee that was setting up the senior prom, and Bonnie was their adviser.

Two of the girls slid into the booth on each side of us, and the other two pulled chairs up out of it, and for the next thirty minutes they talked about decorations, the band they wanted, and a multitude of other details. One of the girls had an iPad (new idea for me) with her, and she was in charge of making notes.

Watching Bonnie with the girls and how much she loved them and they loved her, I thought it was sad that she never had children of her own. I knew she said all the kids in town, even the grownup ones, were her children, so maybe that was all she ever wanted. Bonnie had been so young when she first started teaching. And now these girls were old enough to be her grandchildren.

I did know that Bonnie had come to Whispering Pines to take the job at the school when she was just twenty-two, and I had met her five years later. But I knew nothing about her life before that. Why didn't I know more? Was it just me, or did no one know?

Once the girls walked away, full of purpose and yelling over their shoulders, "Thank you, Miss Bonnie," the discussion about Jack was too far away to bring up again. But that didn't mean I wouldn't pursue it on my own. He seemed a little too young for Bonnie, but that really didn't matter if he would make her happy. That was the part that needed to be determined.

Twenty Six

The next morning, I stopped off at a local coffee shop that I had spotted the other day on our drive into town, got two coffees with crazy names, and headed to the local garden co-op.

I had texted Faye and asked if we could talk, and she said she could, but I'd have to come to her where she was working. Then she requested that I bring her a coffee. Not just a coffee, but the one with a long list of words. In order to buy it, I had to write all the words down and hand them to the coffee guy, who I learned was now called a barista. Fancy name for a coffee guy.

Because I was opening new doors in my life after keeping mine shut for so long, I got myself the same drink too. When I took a sip on the way to the car, I thought it was like drinking dessert. Which was not a bad thing at all.

I found Faye walking through the gardens, looking like both a gardener and a fairy at the same time. She had a trowel in one hand, and I imagined that in the other hand was a magic wand. The fact that she was wearing overalls didn't ruin the fairy look, probably because there were twigs and sprigs of green sticking out of almost every pocket.

As we walked back to the building at the front of the garden, she explained that locals rented the plots, and in the summer, they filled them with vegetables and flowers of all kinds.

When she pointed out her plot, it didn't surprise me to see that green sprouts were everywhere. It had a tiny bench in the middle, and I could picture her sitting there in the summer with her plant friends.

Meetings and classes took place in an old brick building with big windows. It had restrooms for the gardeners, so they could stay as long as they wished. I remember coming to classes there with Harry as we learned about things that he already knew, but he said there was always something new to learn. That was Harry, always exploring.

We settled onto a bench and stared out at the space. Even though the gardens were mostly empty, they were still beautiful, orderly, and peaceful. I could almost hear the rustle of plants beneath the soil as it warmed in the sun.

Off to one side of the plots were small stands of trees with tables under them and a path that curled out into the woods that lay behind the gardens. Bird houses of all kinds dotted the landscape, and with the amount of bird song I was hearing, I knew there were many more birds around than I was seeing.

"Who pays for all this?" I asked, waving my hand at the well-kept building and paths.

Faye looked at me as if I had lost my mind, and then, her face softening, she reached out and held my hand as she said, "You and Harry do."

Now I was sure. I had lost my mind. The visions, losing memories about the past—this was it. My third act in life wouldn't be filled with new things but instead be a loss of everything.

I couldn't help myself. Tears filled my eyes, I looked away, but of course Faye knew. She put both our coffees on the table beside the bench, turned to me, and held me by the shoulders.

"Listen to me. No, you haven't lost your mind, Mabel. And no, you aren't sick. That you can't remember some things makes total sense.

"When Harry died, you wanted to go with him. That didn't work out, did it? You managed to forget, but only because you didn't want to remember. Not because you can't."

Faye's hands on me gave the sensation of being plugged into an electric outlet. I could feel warmth from her hands move down my arms, through my body, down my legs and then into the ground, where it spread out like roots. I felt a jolt, and I was different. It was as if the part of myself that had been living outside of me had returned.

It was good that Faye had taken my coffee away, because otherwise it would have spilled as I let out an oomph and then, collapsing onto Faye, began crying.

Faye said nothing. She just let me cry. And when I was done, she took a tissue from one of her pockets and dabbed my eyes.

"Feel better now?" she asked, her deep blue eyes sparkling.

I nodded, and Faye handed me my coffee, picked up hers, and turned to look at the gardens as if nothing had happened. I leaned back on the bench and looked at the world around me as if I had just woken from a long nap.

There was nothing to say because there was too much to say. Long minutes passed filled with birdsong, lilac-scented breezes, and the occasional chatter from the people working their plots, and I drank it all in. Life was a beautiful gift, and I had been wanting to leave it for too long.

Tipping my head back to look at the blue sky filled with puffy white clouds, I watched two black birds dipping and diving with the air currents. I wondered if they were Jay and Dove. It wouldn't have surprised me if they were.

Finally, I turned to Faye, who smiled at me as I said, "Thank you for bringing me home again."

Yes, I had been remembering little bits of things since the memory book hadn't shown up seven days ago. But I knew now that I had been living like what James Joyce had said about one of his characters, "Mr. Duffy lived a short distance from his body." And now I wasn't.

Returning was not a completely pleasant experience. I seemed to have aches in places where I didn't recall aching before. Of course, that was probably because I wasn't taking care of myself. The body that carried me through the world deserved more attention than I had given it.

"Do you remember all of it?" Faye asked.

"I'm not sure."

"Then perhaps we should go down memory lane together. Tell me what you remember after you came home and fixed up the house. Do you remember what happened after Harry visited and found you here?"

I nodded. I did.

I smiled, closed my eyes and let myself go back to that day.

Twenty Seven

T aking a deep breath and keeping my eyes closed for a moment, I told Faye more about what happened when Harry returned. Of course she had been there, and witnessed it from the outside, and I had probably shared some of this with her, but I couldn't remember if I had or not.

Besides, this was about me piecing my memories back together. As Faye sipped her coffee and we both looked out over the allotments, I let the story unfold.

After our meeting in the woods and spending a few days together, getting to know the grownup versions of ourselves and reliving our childhood, Harry had to return to his book tour.

Although we had only touched the surface of our memories, our talks together while walking in the woods and sitting by the lake were enough to keep us talking while he toured.

He'd call every few days and tell me about the city he was in and the people he'd met. I'd sit in the kitchen at the table I had before Harry got me the tree table and stare into the woods, trying to imagine his life.

Even though I had loved my city life and my city job, now that I had returned home, I knew I could never go back to them. I wasn't sure if Harry could give up his wandering ways, though, so for me, the calls were heaven and hell at the same time.

I knew I had never stopped loving Harry, but I believed that wasn't true for him. I didn't even know if he had loved me in the first place. After all, the last time he saw me was when I was ten, and he was a teenage boy. How could he have loved me then?

But for me, Harry had been my first, and really only, love. I had resigned myself to accepting that I was not his. After dad and I moved away, Harry had built an entire life that had nothing to do with me.

True, he hadn't married, but maybe it was only because he hadn't found the right person yet. Plus, I knew him. He was always wondering about something. What if he had wondered about the many varieties of women?

With all my heart, I wanted him to love me just enough to want to stay, at least some of the time. But I couldn't ask him to leave what I saw as a glamorous life as an author writing books that ended up in bookstores with a huge picture of him on the back cover. His publisher sent him all over the world. He was interviewed on TV. He was a star.

That was my perception of Harry and his life. But as the weeks went by and he called me from the road, I learned the other side of his life. And I knew there was a chance that he could eventually choose Whispering Pines and me. Or at least make me his home base.

After a few months, the tour was over, and he came to visit again. That time, it was different. Instead of staying in the one tiny motel we had in Whispering Pines, he stayed with me. I had transformed the house by then, and my childhood bedroom was my grown-up bedroom.

I kept it because I could look out the window and see his old house. One morning, Harry asked me why I had made my bedroom the one that looked out over the street rather than the one that looked out over the garden and woods.

My answer was that now that he was in my bedroom, perhaps I could make that change. Harry waited a long beat, looked at me, the house across the street, and I could see he understood something he hadn't fully known before.

Later that day, we made the change. We moved to the bedroom that used to be my parents room, where we could see the trees swaying in the wind. Eventually my old bedroom would become Jenny's. But I never saw her staring at the house across the street as I had done.

It was presumptuous of me to move the bedroom, thinking that perhaps it would convince Harry to stay, but I did it for him. He wanted the trees.

The days flew by. I refused to think about the day he would leave again, because I knew he would. He spent the days clacking away at his next book on the electric typewriter he traveled with. I hoped that if he was happy writing in my house, he wouldn't have to go back home to write. I spent the days taking care of the house and watching over him.

The day before he left to return to his home and yet another book tour, we went for a last walk in the woods behind his old house. I was afraid. He was so somber. I prepared myself for him telling me he wouldn't be coming back.

I held my breath when he turned to me. Harry, who was charming and outgoing when speaking to a group of people, was quiet and almost wordless when he wasn't. He said he used up all his energy speaking to people and it took time for him to get it back.

He barely spoke this time, either. No flowery words, nothing to prepare me, just a simple, "Mabel Stone will you marry me?"

Hearing those words, words I had never dared to dream he would say—only wished it with all my heart—turned me into a frozen statue.

I stopped breathing. Harry waited, holding my hands.

Later, he told me he had been terrified that I was going to break his heart. Instead, mine had burst open and forced my entire body to pause for a moment and take in the dream come true.

Finally, my breath returned, and I started laughing and saying, "Yes, yes, yes!" and jumped into his arms and held on.

We spun around and around. The trees swayed with us, birds sang, and a squirrel sat up on a log beside us and told us how happy he was for us. The world stopped and it became just the two of us.

As I told Faye this story, tears streamed down her face, matching mine. Here we were, two old women sitting on a bench crying over love. *But then, what better thing to cry over,* I thought.

"Had you forgotten that moment, Mabel?" Faye asked

"That I could never forget," I answered, but as I said it, I realized I had.

Not the moment, but the feeling. Over the years, I never stopped loving Harry, but life kicked in, and Harry kept disappearing, so part of me was frustrated with him. And then I was angry with myself for being frustrated, because I had always known that Harry was a wanderer.

But I could always count on his love for me, and that he would return, bringing gifts and stories. Of course this last trip for him was not one he could return from. Instead, I would have to follow him there.

But it wasn't time yet, and I finally fully realized that I was very happy that was true.

What I didn't tell Faye was that now that I was remembering, I was remembering something else. Harry had a secret. One that he told me before he died. And for some reason, it had frightened me.

Why I was frightened, I didn't remember. But I did remember it was why I had stayed home, hidden away, forgetting my place in the world, because Harry had left me with the secret and I didn't want it. I guess I thought that if I ignored it it would go away.

But it hadn't. Even now, in the sunshine of a beautiful May day, I could feel its dark shadow, waiting for me to acknowledge it.

I wasn't ready.

Twenty Eight

Harry's secret, the one I was trying to remember but not remember at the same time, stopped the words from coming out of my mouth. Instead, vague pictures swirled in my head.

It was like looking into a mist and seeing a shape but not knowing what it was. It could be something scary, or it could be something innocent. Until the mist clears and reveals what is hidden, fear stays.

That's how I felt. I didn't know if what Harry had told me should make me afraid or not, but because I didn't remember, I was afraid.

Faye was patiently waiting for me to continue, but then I knew I couldn't. Not right at that moment.

"Let's return to my story later. Right now, I want to talk about Bonnie."

Faye nodded, not needing more of an explanation. "Peggy has you wondering about Jack."

"Shouldn't we know more about him?"

Faye paused, looked around at the allotments, which had started to fill up with more people, and said, "Why not just ask her?"

"I did. She deflected the question."

"Well, let's find out on our own, shall we?"

What a good idea, I thought. *Finding out who Jack was would be like uncovering a secret. One that couldn't possibly be as scary as the one I would have to uncover about Harry.*

At that moment, Faye's replacement showed up, and we were free to go.

"Where do you suggest we go to find out?" I asked.

"You need some work done on your house, don't you?"

It was true. I did. I had let it go into disrepair. Things needed to be fixed, updated, and painted. I could think of a long list of things that needed to be done. Besides, Fix the House was on my to-do list.

"What's that got to do with Jack?"

"Jack works for a construction company. Let's go talk to him."

So off we went. Me in my new clothes, and Faye in her overalls, with a few plants still sticking out of them. I loved her for it.

Jack wasn't there. He was off checking on a construction site, but he'd be back in an hour. Did we want to come back? Or could someone else help us?

Faye smiled at the huge, stern man standing in front of her, and he melted. It was something I had witnessed over and over through the years. I thought it was good that Faye never used that superpower for evil. She could have ruled the world.

She said we'd be back in an hour to talk to Jack because he had come highly recommended.

As we walked out, I whispered, "Who recommended him?"

"Bonnie, of course."

I snort laughed. Of course she did. We ate a quick lunch at the same diner we had come to last time. I had discovered they made great grilled cheese, and Faye liked the huge garden salad they served.

But this time being at the diner was a completely different experience than the one just a few days before. I saw people do a double take when Faye and I walked in. Then, realizing it was me, all spruced up, smiled. I guess they liked what they saw. And this time I waved and smiled at everyone in return, even though I still didn't know who they were. But I felt that I did and that made a huge difference.

After our quick but delicious lunch, we returned to find Jack sitting in an office that was way too neat for a construction site.

He noticed us glancing around and said, "I need things in order to think."

Although Jack hadn't meant it as a learning lesson, I realized that I did too. No wonder I had been a little hazy about things. My house was not in order.

Surprisingly, Jack recognized us from the line dancing lessons and asked if we were coming back. Faye said we were, even though, up until then, I hadn't planned to return. And then, smiling her charming smile, she asked Jack why and when he had started dancing,.

His answer was that he wasn't really a dancer, but his mother and father had always loved to dance, and doing something this simple was his nod to his parents.

"Besides, it's fun, don't you think?"

"And you don't need a partner," Faye added. I recognized it as a hint, but Jack didn't, or pretended that he didn't. He just smiled, nodded, and asked what he could do for us.

As I explained my house and what I thought I would need, Jack opened an account for me on his computer and then took notes on his iPad. He said it helped him remember what questions to ask once he got to my house.

After explaining to Jack what I thought needed to be done in the house, he scheduled an appointment with me in the morning to walk through everything. After that, he'd figure out what it would cost and make a list of what I wanted done first.

Jack was nice, efficient, and just charming enough to make me feel comfortable with my decision. I didn't get any strange feelings about him. However, I still couldn't see why Bonnie seemed so interested in him. He didn't seem to be her type.

What her type was, I didn't know since I had never seen her date, but still, something didn't feel right. But maybe it wasn't about Jack. Maybe it was about something else.

However, I did need my house fixed up. And it would give me plenty of opportunities to learn more about Jack and his history. All of which was necessary before I gave my "approval" for Bonnie's interest in him.

As Faye and I walked back to her car, it occurred to me that it could all be one-sided. Bonnie was interested in Jack. But he wasn't interested in her, other than as someone he had met. At the moment, it seemed that was what it was.

When I said as much to Faye, she agreed. So why was Bonnie so interested in him? Was he a past student? Bonnie never forgot a student. I'd have to ask Jack where he grew up when I saw him in the morning.

I knew I could just ask him about Bonnie, but if I did it wrong, it could ruin my relationship with Bonnie. I wasn't willing to risk that for anything. All I wanted to do was make sure Bonnie was safe and happy.

But I knew it was more than that. I had the sense that whatever Harry had told me before he walked into the woods to die was somehow tied to Jack.

And as afraid as I was to find out, I was equally afraid not to.

Twenty Nine

The next morning, before Grace arrived, I had eaten the last of the croissants for breakfast and gone for a short walk with Jay and Dove. Grace had been with her mom the day before, getting ready to go to work at the summer camp.

I was just filling her in on what Faye and I had done when she wasn't around when Jack pulled up in his truck.

"Hey, that's Jack White," Grace said, looking out the window. "What's he doing here? Oh, I bet you are getting your house fixed up. That's so cool!"

I stared at Grace. She was happy to see this guy. What was going on?

"You know him?"

"Sure. He's dating mom."

Grace didn't wait to see my expression; she was up, and at the door to let him in before I could gather my thoughts. All I could think was, *Poor Bonnie.*

I heard, rather than saw, Jack ask Grace what she was doing there, and I only looked up when she said, "Yes, this is my Gammy."

Seeing Jack go pale, I figured Jenny had told him about her mother, and it probably wasn't all that kind. But he recovered quickly and came over to shake my hand.

"You should have said. Or I should have figured it out. But then you have different last names. But still. I am delighted to be here. "

And then, realizing that if he hadn't known who I was, I also hadn't known about him dating Jenny, he paused.

An awkward moment passed as we both processed what we hadn't known. Grace rescued us by jabbering on how excited she was that he would be fixing up her grandmother's house.

To Jack's credit, he seemed to like Grace, and she obviously liked him, and that earned him quite a few points. However, I decided I would have to take it up with Grace as to why she hadn't told me about him before.

But then I realized that wasn't fair. We avoided the subject of her mother as much as possible. I did it because I didn't want to put Grace in the position of choosing sides, and she probably kept information to herself out of respect for her mother and a sense of kindness to me.

Grace walked with me and Jack through the house as he made notes. It was good that she was there because she pointed out things I hadn't noticed. Some were small, like a loose stair banister, and some were larger, like the wet spot above the shower in my bathroom.

When we were done, Jack said, "This is an extensive list. What do you want to get done first? And I'm sorry to ask, but it's going to be expensive. Will you be able to do it all?

Once again, I was grateful to both Harry and my father. Dad's money would have been enough for me to live on for the rest of my life, but Harry had money, too. And an insurance policy. Both men in my life had made sure I would be taken care of. Tears came to my eyes at the thought of their love for me, and Jack misinterpreted them.

"It's okay. We'll do only what's necessary."

I assured him that money wasn't a problem, and again, with Grace's help, we made a plan, starting with a new roof. Once he had seen the one leak, Jack found more leaks, and I realized my house had been leaking for some time. *Like me*, I thought.

As he turned to leave, Jack said, "I'll take point on this, Miss Mabel."

For some reason, when he called me Miss Mabel, it clinched the deal for me. There was nothing wrong with Jack. Which didn't mean that there wasn't something wrong with Bonnie and her interest in him.

As he turned to leave, I called after him and asked if he knew anyone who could clear the path in my woods. I explained that my husband had made it for me, but it was now overgrown.

"I know the perfect person," he said. "I'll have him call you. His name is Pete. He has the perfect last name for what he does. Pete Woods."

Grace had to leave too; she had work. But before she left, she turned to hug me.

"I'm so happy you are fixing up the house, Gammy. I was worried about leaving you here while I go off to work at the camp and then school."

It was then that I realized, once again, how selfish I had been. Not intentionally. But shutting down the way I had must have been hard on all the people around me. It had never occurred to me.

"I'll be okay, Grace. In fact, I have a list of things to do."

Grace smiled. The smile reminded me of Harry, and I thought again of how lucky I was to have her.

As Grace opened her car door, she called out, "Come to lunch?"

I gave her a thumbs up. Why not?

After watching her drive away, I sat in my comfy chair and pulled out my list to see where I was with it.

- Do something to help the town.

Well, I guess I was already doing that, according to Faye, but I wanted to find out more about that. Where else was I giving money, and who set it up? I assumed Harry, but then who was managing it?

If it were me, I couldn't be doing a very good job of it. Time to improve.

- Clean up my garden.

Yes, I could start on that, but I needed help. I'd ask Faye if she knew someone at the allotments who would help me. Luckily, I had lots of money to fling around, so no one would have to work for free.

- Clear the paths in the woods.

Pete Woods would take care of that. I wondered, with a name like that, if he looked like a tree. For some reason, that thought cracked me up, and I giggled my way through the rest of the list.

- Talk to people.

Yep. I was doing that. I needed to do more of it. Maybe I could strike up a conversation or two at the restaurant. Bring Peggy; that would help.

- Help Bonnie.

This one was tricky. Did she know Jack was dating my daughter? Did Peggy or Faye? I'd find out.

- Find out more about Faye, Bonnie, and Peggy's lives.

This one was in process. More talking, more asking questions, and more listening were necessary.

- Fix the bird feeders and get bird food.

I'd ask Jack about fixing the bird feeders and have Grace get bird food the next time she went shopping for me.

Yes, I was moving along with my list. But what I hadn't put on the list was probably the most necessary.

- Remember what Harry told me before he died.

I was getting there, but I also knew I was avoiding it. Maybe by putting it on my list, that would help. Then I remembered Jack's orderly office, so I added another item to my list.

- Put my house in order.

That entailed quite a bit. Stuff needed to be thrown away or given away. But not just that house. My mental house. And maybe by doing that, I would remember what I had forgotten. Not just what Harry had told me, but also the skills that my friends kept alluding to.

That's enough of that, I said to myself, and I texted Peggy, asking if she wanted to go to lunch.

"Be there in thirty," she texted back.

While I waited, I let myself drift away. A little nap was a good thing.

As I breathed in and out slowly, I let the mist return and wash over me. This time it was a soft blue, and it stirred up memories just enough for me to know they were there.

I heard Harry's voice as I drifted deeper. "Remember the magic, Mabel."

And for a moment, I did.

Thirty

As usual, Peggy was right on time. She pulled into the driveway and honked her horn, announcing to the world that she was there.

Not waiting for me to come out of the house, she flung open the door of her car and stepped out to come get me. With her bright red nail polish and lipstick that matched her bright red pants and a green tunic, she looked exactly like a walking tulip.

That thought made me laugh and love her more than ever. For seventy-five years, Peggy Sue Smith had made the world a brighter place to live in, and I figured she'd be at it until the day she died. Given her love of life, she could last forever.

She knew why I was laughing. Glancing down at her outfit, she gestured to it as she bowed. "You like?"

"More than like. Love!"

"You don't look so bad either, my little magical fairy friend."

I smiled and told her Grace was responsible for my renewed look, but her words struck a cord. I thought of Faye as the magical fairy friend. Did Peggy have me mixed up with her, or were Faye and I more alike than I remembered?

Over lunch, tucked back in a private corner where Grace had seated us without us asking, and after Peggy made her trip around the restaurant, saying hi to almost everyone there, I filled her in on what had happened the last few days.

When I got to the part where I discovered that Jack was dating Jenny, Peggy slapped her forehead so loudly that half the restaurant glanced over at us. Obviously, she hadn't known.

"Maybe we misinterpreted Bonnie's interest in Jack?" I suggested.

Peggy's "I suppose that's possible" didn't ring true at all.

Besides, I knew Peggy better than that. She might look like a tulip, but when she got hold of something, she was like a pit bull. She wasn't done with the Jack problem. And she wouldn't be until she solved the mystery of why Bonnie was staring at him like that.

"Line dancing tomorrow night?" Peggy said. "We'll do what we did last time. We'll all go out to eat and then go dancing."

I agreed. It wouldn't do any good to argue with Peggy. Besides, I had to admit I had fun, and it was on my list after all to get to know my friends better.

In the meantime, I would look for the magic memory book. I had just accepted that it hadn't shown up this year. Maybe I hadn't looked in the right place. And even if I didn't find it, I would actively work at remembering without it.

Deciding to remember something and actually remembering it are at least two different things. Besides, I knew memory was always false. No matter what I remembered, it wouldn't be what really happened. The only accurate memory is the one that happens as it happens. In the moment.

And that itself was iffy since we only saw what we expected to see. It made me wonder if anything I thought or saw was real.

Because after something happens, the memory of it is a creative act. Remembering how we wanted it to be, thought it was, or were afraid of what it was. So even though I was actively pursuing a memory that I had stored in a vault in my mind, I knew it might not be true. In fact, it probably wasn't.

Still, there was a feeling. And since that morning, when the memory book didn't show up, that feeling had been clinging to me. Sometimes it was a light touch, like sunlight on my face. Other times, it felt like something was tugging at me, and I was actively resisting it.

After Peggy dropped me off at home, honking as she drove away, waving at me, and then at the people who lived across the street, I spent time looking for the memory book.

Every anniversary of Harry's birthday, when I came downstairs, it had always just been sitting on the side table beside the chair. Waiting. But thinking back, I couldn't actually say what it looked like.

Looking back, it seemed that each time it was a different color and a different shape. Which, of course, was impossible. Realizing that I didn't even know what the memory book looked like made me wonder if perhaps it had never been there.

Had I just come downstairs each morning on Harry's birthday and imagined it? Had I opened an imaginary book and studied it, remembering the best parts of our lives together?

If so, then there was nothing to look for. Instead, I could pretend, since I thought it was possible; that's what I had been doing all along. Pretending.

For sure, I had been pretending to be living a life when really I had shut down everything important to me. Only Grace had kept me going. Now that I was awake, or waking up from that self-induced isolation, I decided that it was my choice to remember what I wanted to.

And if I made up parts of it, what would it matter? So I made myself a cup of tea instead of coffee, thinking that doing something a little different than usual might help the process. I settled down in my comfy chair and thought of Shakespeare's quote, "and perhaps to dream." And waited.

Nothing happened. I couldn't even fall asleep. I reached into the drawer and took out the picture book Grace had made for me. I flipped to the empty pages at the end of the book and started writing.

I started with after Harry asked me to marry him. At that moment, it had felt as if the heavens had opened up and showered me with pink rose petals and serenaded us with angels singing. For the next few days, we lived in a magic world of our own making. Only thinking of each other. Barely talking about the future, because the present was so wonderful.

For a few days, we both forgot there was a world outside of us, one that would make demands on each of us and, in truth, do its best to pull us apart. We forgot about everything except how glorious it was to be in love.

And then the day came when Harry had to leave again.

But before he left, he had made arrangements for everything he owned to be packed up and brought to what is now our house in Whispering Pines. So even though he was gone, his stuff came to me, and he gave me permission to unpack everything and arrange it the way I wanted to.

It wasn't much, really. Harry had always rented furnished places, saying he didn't need to own a lot since he was always on the move.

He mostly had books. So while he was away, I had book shelves installed on both sides of the fireplace. Looking up from my writing, I looked at the rows of Harry's books that still lived on those bookshelves.

Before Harry came home, I arranged them one way. But when Harry returned, after thanking me for the bookshelves, he arranged them another way. I could never figure out the order of what he had done. So if I wanted to read a specific book, I had to ask him where it was.

He always knew. He'd walk over and grab it without even skimming the titles. After I was done reading it, I'd give it back to him, and he'd put it back where it belonged.

Looking at the books again, I still couldn't see the order. I thought it looked like a bunch of random colors. And then I had a wild thought. The books looked like one of those magic eye pictures. The kind where you unfocus your eyes one way and focus them another, and a picture pops out that had been there all along.

Thinking I had nothing to lose, I pretended that the bookshelf on the right of the fireplace was a magic eye image, and within a few moments, something started to appear. I was so shocked, I lost it. But it was there. I knew it was there; all I had to do was relax and look again.

And then there it was. A picture Harry had been seeing all along.

Thirty One

My ability to see the hidden picture on the bookshelf lasted for only a few breaths. I was so astonished at what had happened that I lost focus, and it was gone. Nothing I did to make it come back worked. I knew I was trying too hard.

Relax, I kept telling myself, which only made it worse.

All I knew was that the books had disappeared and there was a picture of something. Just like a magic eye picture. And just like many magic-eye pictures, the scene was not a normal picture. Everything was floating around.

I thought there were birds, maybe a tree, maybe a house, maybe a canoe. All of which Harry would have liked. But why arrange books to look that way?

Was Harry able to see the hidden picture all the time? How had he figured out how to do that? What did it mean? And was it not really there? Was it just another version of me possibly losing my mind?

And if it was there, why did Harry make it? It was so complicated. How had he pulled it off? I had no answers, only questions, and a mixture of awe, confusion, and, once again, anger.

All the years we had lived in our house together, Harry had never told me about the bookshelves or the hidden pictures. That was assuming that I actually saw them and wasn't going crazy. I also had to assume the other bookshelf contained a picture too, because to me, the books were also just a jumbled mass of books of all shapes, sizes, and colors.

Looking at the bookshelves now, I wondered why I hadn't made him explain why they were that way. But I had accepted it because, well, it was Harry. It didn't hurt me, and it pleased him.

Did he think I would never discover the hidden reason for the way he had arranged them? Or had he put them there, waiting for the day I would discover them?

Perhaps he thought he would be alive when it happened. Then we would have celebrated together, and he would have hugged me and swung me around, as he had done that day in the woods.

Maybe he had waited patiently for me to insist on telling me why the books were that way. Or perhaps the pictures weren't for me at all. Perhaps they were always meant to be a secret. Or was it a joke? Or a message? Was it for me or for someone else?

And if it were for someone else, then who? We didn't have many guests at our house. The only people that were in our house were Jenny, Grace, my three friends, and perhaps Jenny's friends when she lived there. We enjoyed keeping our house as our cozy nest. Neither of us were entertainers. If we wanted a party, it would be somewhere else.

So if the pictures weren't for me and they weren't for a person who came into the house, then Harry had even more secrets than I thought.

I wanted to cry, scream, and laugh, all at the same time. But most of all, I wanted Harry.

I wanted to have him sit in the other chair in the living room. The one just like mine. The one that faced the fireplace but could swivel so we could face each other when we talked, or swivel to look out the window at the house across the street.

That's what I wanted. I wanted Harry so much that I couldn't breathe. But the anger at him for his secrets and his leaving me made it impossible for me to think straight. How dare he leave me? Why hadn't he told me he was dying? Why hadn't he told me he was going to the woods to let himself drift away?

I had made up my own reasons for his actions. I had decided that it was probably because he knew that I would have begged him to stay, but he couldn't. But I had been barely functioning without him.

Sure, I saw him once in a while. He would stand at the foot of my bed in the morning, or wait by the path in the woods by the lake, even sitting in his chair as if he were going to start one of our wonderful talks.

But he wasn't really in my life in the old way. I couldn't hold his hands or go to the movies with him. He couldn't call me and tell me he loved me. He couldn't dry the dishes while I washed or drive me to the store so we could shop together.

And I wondered how anyone went on when the love of their life wasn't there anymore. *People must do it,* I told myself. *But how?*

By the time I had recovered enough from a bout of anger and weeping, feeling sorry for myself and angry because I was feeling sorry for myself, it was evening.

I put the picture book with my writing in the drawer of the side table and stood. Everything creaked. I had been in the chair for too long. As I closed the front curtains, I said, "Good night, Harry," as I had said for so many years as a child to the boy across the street. Now I said it to the man who was no longer there and never would be again.

As I made my way upstairs to bed, I reminded myself that I had things to do the next day. Important things. Friends to help. A house to repair. A garden to plant. And a mystery to solve.

But what was the picture I saw on the bookshelves? What had Harry told me I couldn't remember? What did I used to do that people seemed to expect of me?

And maybe finally, I should do what I should have done years before: find out where Harry went when he traveled. Book tours? All those book tours? Is that what he was doing, or was it something else?

Thirty Two

As I was making my way upstairs to bed, I looked at the house differently. Were there more magic-eye pictures hidden throughout the house? Was anything arranged to be a picture if I looked again?

I doubted it. Other than the bookshelves that Harry had rearranged, I was responsible for where everything else was placed. When I returned home from Los Angeles, I had designed the house to be cozy-chic. Later, when Harry moved in, his stuff had barely made a dent.

Cozy-chic was probably what my mother had been going for, because when I found a picture of what cozy-chic looked like in a magazine, I realized that's what the house already looked like. All the house needed was sprucing up, which helped me feel closer to her.

Most of the furniture in the house was still what I had grown up with. Over the years, I had each piece repaired and refurbished. Then, if I wanted to buy something new, it had to pass a few tests. First, it had to be comfortable. Then it had to match the rest of the house. And last but not least, I asked the item if it wanted to come home with me or not.

It was an odd thing to ask an inanimate piece of furniture, but I always heard the answer. Everything in the house wanted to be there. But did it still? Things had changed. I had changed.

As I cautiously took one step at a time up to my bedroom, I had to ask myself if I belonged in my house anymore. But I didn't wait for the answer because, honestly, I didn't want to hear it.

Instead, I cursed my way up the stairs, and when I reached the top, I paused and looked around. There were too many rooms in my house for one person. How had I not noticed that before?

I guess in my mind's eye, I always thought that Harry and I would live in the house until we both died. Then Jenny and Grace would inherit the house and do what they wanted with it. I had never let myself think about anything past that. And now that Harry was gone, I had a big house with just me in it.

A few ideas of how to make use of the house better came to mind. Maybe the girls—meaning Faye, Bonnie, and Peggy—could come to live with me. As I laid out my clothes and put on my nightgown, I imagined how much fun that would be. And then I laughed out loud, seeing what that would look like.

Sure, for a day or two, it would be fun, and then it would be terrible. We were all set in our ways, having lived on our own for years. Bonnie and Faye never married; Peggy had left her last husband over twenty years ago, and now I had been alone for eleven years.

As I fell asleep, I was still laughing to myself at the sight of all of us living together. The last thing I remembered was Harry whispering that it was time to move on. And me saying "no." And meaning, "Yes, I know it is."

That night, I had the weirdest dream. I dreamed I was floating in a sea of vastness. Everything in the world was around me. Impossible, of course, but not in a dream.

Harry had once shown me that a photo was comprised of millions of pixels. And in my dream, that's how I saw everything in the world. Everything is comprised of pixels. Including myself.

In the dream, how the world around me appeared depended on how my eyes were focused. Focused one way, everything was solid. Looking at it differently, everything in the world was made up of pixels.

When I awoke, for a split second, the world was still pixelated, and then the image was gone and the world was solid again. *Like a magic eye picture*, I thought to myself.

Before Grace arrived in the morning, I made notes about what I wanted to talk to her about. I didn't want to chicken out and not ask her. And perhaps it was asking too much of an eighteen-year-old, but Grace had always been more grownup than her age.

When she was little, she made us give her a birthday party and declare that she was twelve when she was only six. Her explanation was that time was not measured in years, and she could be whatever age she wished to be.

With that kind of reasoning, we all had to agree with her. So, by Grace's standards, she was definitely old enough to help me with what needed to be done.

When I sat her down and told her about my list, she agreed to do whatever she could. But when I told her the first few items on my list, she sat back and stared at me.

Are you sure, Gammy?

I assured her I was. I needed to find someone to help me sell the house and buy something more appropriate for me. I had a long list of what that might look like, and I think Grace thought I would never find that, anyway.

But I knew I would. We both decided to ask Jack for a recommendation, or my accountant. I said those words, knowing I couldn't remember ever meeting with an accountant. Things had always been taken care of for me. Even after Harry had died. The fact that I had let all of those things slip out of my head made me angry with myself.

And I let that anger fuel me as Grace and I started the search for Harry's papers. Not finding any, I stopped and thought about what Faye had said. She knew I was giving money to the allotments. What else did she know?

Grace placed the call to Faye because I was still fuming. I had heard once that depression was anger turned on oneself. Well, now that I didn't feel depressed, I suppose that anger had to go somewhere. And it was definitely coming out. Because I didn't know how to stop it, I took it as a good sign. I was returning to the land of the living, but I wasn't sure I would be happy about what I was about to discover.

Thirty Three

Faye arrived with a notebook and an accordion file filled with manila file folders and lots of papers.

When Grace greeted her, I swear, a look passed between them. To me, that meant Grace knew all along what Faye had been doing. Probably Grace helped her. Another spark of anger flared up. It was hard to tell who I was the maddest at: myself, Faye, or Grace.

After Faye hugged Grace, she looked at me, and seeing my face, she smiled anyway. I didn't smile back. But when she said, "I have been waiting for this day," all my anger melted away.

Why would I be angry with Faye and Grace for taking care of what needed to be done? If anything, I should be bowing down in gratitude. If I was going to be angry, it would have to be with myself and my decision to shut down, run away, hide, and leave the mess to others to handle.

However, once the anger dissipated, I felt the desire to shut down again. I heard the voice in my head tell me I didn't deserve any of this care and attention. It was familiar and very tempting to listen to it. But this time, instead of giving into it, I unleashed every curse word I knew at that temptation, and it retreated.

I hid the internal struggle and cursing by preparing coffee, so by the time I turned around, I had quieted that voice. I didn't think anyone had noticed, but then, how long had Grace and Faye—and who knew who else—been taking care of an angry, sullen, and withdrawn old woman?

Probably long enough to recognize what I had just done. But they both smiled at me in encouragement, and I smiled back. My smile, a smile that this time came from my heart, was a good sign that I had banished the regrets and fears, at least for the moment.

The three of us sat around the tree table, and Faye opened the notebook and showed me how she had been keeping track of everything.

Her answer to why and how made me want to put my head down, weep, and maybe go back to bed for a week and stop thinking again.

Harry had set it up with her. He had explained that if something happened to him, he worried I wouldn't handle it well. If that happened, he had asked her to step up and take over until I was ready to.

I didn't have to ask Faye why Harry had chosen her. Faye, with all her fairy-like qualities, had a mind that loved numbers and organization. For years, she had worked as an independent bookkeeper for a few accountants in town and for us directly. Of course, I had conveniently forgotten that fact.

Staring at her now, the notebook open on the table, all the papers labeled and organized, I knew I owed her more than I could ever repay. How many years had Faye been making sure I was okay?

It had been Faye who had orchestrated and organized my return to Whispering Pines. It was Faye who held my hand and went for walks with me in the woods when Harry was on one of his trips.

And now I knew it was Faye who had been taking care of all the things I had taken for granted for over eleven years. Those years had flown by as if they were a dream. Where had I been? And why?

A knock on the door interrupted us. The roofers had arrived. Grace went outside to show them where everything was, and while she was gone, I asked Faye the obvious question. "Why? Why do all this?"

And her answer was so Faye.

"Why not? You needed me. Harry asked me. It made me happy."

For my part, I could only stare at my friend. Nothing seemed that easy to me, and I thought she wasn't telling me everything.

Her question to me was just as obvious.

"Are you ready to take over?"

My answer was not so straight-forward. I didn't know. Yet. I had too many questions. About the house. The magic-eye bookcase. Harry's secrets. And had I ever been capable of doing what Faye had been doing? And why had Harry assumed I would fall apart? Had I always been that weak?

So much of it made little sense to me. I used to be a stockbroker, for heaven's sake. A city girl. I was perfectly capable of handling all that Faye had been doing.

Except, obviously, I wasn't.

Thirty Four

Jack arrived a few minutes after the roofers, and after conferring with them to make sure everything was going as planned, he knocked on the door to see how we were doing, and I invited him into the kitchen for coffee.

Faye hid her surprise at seeing him there. Both Grace and I had forgotten to tell her that Jack was the contractor for the work that would happen with the house.

Watching Faye's face, I realized I had neglected to tell her anything about what was happening with the house. And since I really didn't know how much money I had before I made that decision, she should have been the first person to know, even before I started.

But Faye, being Faye, let none of her surprise show. She simply shook his hand and said she had seen him a few nights before when we all went line dancing. He nodded politely, and we realized that although we had noticed him, he hadn't noticed us. Why would he? Which made me worry again about Bonnie, who seemed so taken with him.

I explained to Jack that Faye had been taking care of my affairs, so he could also listen to what Faye needed because she would always represent what I wanted. He asked if Faye had the power of attorney to sign papers, and when I just stared at him, it was Faye who answered that she did.

Reaching across the table, she held my hand and smiled, letting me know she knew I had not realized that she did. But, of course, she had to have had it. Otherwise, how could she have paid the bills and done everything she had done for all these years? Had she always had it? Or had Harry given it to her? How long had I been missing from the world?

Harry was gone physically, but obviously I had been missing, too. Had I been trying to follow him where I couldn't go? Or was it something else?

After a few more minutes of chit-chat, Jack said he had many houses to check on, and he had to run. Since he was in a rush, I didn't want to talk to him about selling my house and enlisting his help to find me another one. It could wait.

Before going, he turned and asked if we would be line dancing that night.

"Yep," Grace answered for us, and she gave him a hug. And then I stood at the door and waved to him as he got into his truck. When she turned back to the room, seeing Faye's face, Grace said, "He's dating my mom."

"But what about Bonnie?" Faye asked.

"What about Bonnie?"

When we explained to Grace what Faye meant, Grace said she was sure that it couldn't be what we thought it was. But it was definitely time to find out why Bonnie was so interested in Jack. We'd use dinner and line dancing to find out more.

After the two of them left, I was busy the rest of the day with the house. Pete Woods showed up, and although he didn't actually look like a tree, he did look like he lived with them for a long time.

I had envisioned a young man, but instead, he was probably as old as me. It was hard to tell with his tanned and lined face.

I showed him the entrance to the path in the woods, and soon he was busy with chainsaws clearing the way. He unloaded a tractor off the trailer behind his truck, drove it back through the now nonexistent garden, and started moving what he was clearing out into a pile.

Seeing the pile of limbs and bushes accumulating in the yard and watching the pieces of old roofing fall to the ground, I had to remind myself that a mess often needed to be made in order to make things better. I didn't want to think about the mess in my head that needed to be cleared up before things could be better. But I knew it had to happen.

Between Pete and the roofers, the noise was overwhelming, and I realized I had to get away from it. At that moment, Jay tapped on the window, and I knew he couldn't take the noise any longer either. It was time for a walk. I went out the kitchen door into the backyard, waited for Pete to turn off his saw, and told him where I was going. He nodded and said he'd be a while, so he'd watch over things while I was gone.

If he noticed that a raven was walking with me, he didn't say. Perhaps he was like Faye and took those kinds of things for granted.

As for me, I realized I had been taking too many things for granted for too many years. I mentally ran over my to-do list and gave myself a thumbs up for what I had accomplished so far.

Once again, I waved at my neighbors and smiled as we walked to the lake, and I realized how much better I felt when I did that. I was rejoining the land of the living.

As Jay and I entered the woods around the lake, me walking and Jay flying ahead, I saw a blur, and then Harry was standing ahead of me on the trail. He smiled, waved, and then was gone. I wished he would have stayed so I could ask him questions, but at least I knew he was still watching over me.

It was probably small-minded and selfish of me to ask for more than that. Still, I was happy to see him, if only for a moment. And then he was gone, as always, and I realized I was both happy to see him and angry. Again.

But this time, instead of fighting those feelings or disappearing into forgetfulness, I let them both live together for a minute. And then I smiled up at Jay, shook my head to clear it, and moved into the woods to see what had popped up since the last time I had been here.

It was spring in the woods, and everything was new again. Just like me. Or at least I was budding. Not blooming yet. I was still deciding if I could or not and what kind of bloom I would be when I did.

Thirty Five

The roofers were gone for the day when I got back, and Pete was waiting to leave. Once he was gone, it was quiet enough to take a brief nap, which this time, thankfully, contained no dreams.

When I woke up, I had a few hours before dinner, so I used the time to clean out my closet. First, I picked up what I was going to wear to dinner and dancing. Then I started on the closet. When I finished, there were two huge piles of old clothes stacked on my bed.

Looking at the piles of clothes that I didn't want, it was obvious how dark and dreary I had let myself become. What was left in my closet were a few pieces Harry had loved, and my new clothes, which Grace had helped me pick out. I had lots of closet space for new clothes, but I didn't want to buy more because if I was going to move, I didn't want to have to move them.

Glancing in the full-length mirror leaning in the corner of my bedroom, I could see that the woman standing there was an entirely different one than the woman from just a week before. That woman had barely dragged herself down the stairs that day.

And the only reason she was even a little excited then was that it was the day for the memory book.

The memory book was still missing, but the old me, the one I had put away like a used rag, was returning, and I kind of liked her. I said hello to the new-old me in the mirror and cautiously made my way down the stairs. I was no longer interested in breaking my neck.

Still, as I made my way down, I cursed each step out loud, this time since there was no one around to shush me or to be embarrassed. I stopped cursing when it occurred to me it wasn't the steps' fault. They had always been there. It was my fault for letting myself get so weak. So, instead, for the last few steps, I cursed myself.

I knew what I had to do, and it belonged on my list. I had copied my to-do list and put it in my purse so I wouldn't forget. Once I safely reached the bottom of the steps, I pulled the list out and added, "Get stronger."

I didn't care how it happened. I could take a class, go to a gym, work in the garden, or hire someone to come to the house to walk me through exercises. *Just do it*, I said to myself.

Before folding the list and returning it to my purse, I read it out loud to myself. I thought that would help me remember.

- Do something to help the town.

- Clean up my garden.

- Clear the paths in the woods.

- Talk to people.

- Help Bonnie.

- Find out more about Faye, Bonnie, and Peggy's lives.

- Fix the bird feeders and get bird food.

- Fix the house.

- Sell the house and find a place to live.

- Get stronger.

I was pleased with myself because I was doing something towards everything on that list, including getting stronger. I figured going line dancing counted towards getting stronger, and I was talking to people, helping Bonnie, and learning more about Faye, Bonnie, and Peggy's lives.

Dressed and ready to go, I had to wait for Peggy to pick me up. It was feeling like high school all over again. Back then, Peggy would come to get me and take me somewhere to have fun. She would dress to impress and emit enough energy and life to start a fire.

There were always other people in the car, and of course I was always the tag-along. But Peggy had said I was like a sister and she didn't want to leave me behind, and her friends just went along with it. It reminded me of the saying, "Love me, love my dog."

I didn't mind being Peggy's "dog." In fact, I loved it. I knew she dragged me everywhere to put her seal of approval on me and to protect me from the bullies in school.

No one was going to cross Peggy and her massive circle of friends. In Peggy's world, people took care of me. When I got old enough to date, in Peggy's opinion, it was Peggy who supervised who I went out with. Back then, a six year age difference meant something.

Dad had relinquished all responsibility of me to Peggy. Somehow, she had convinced him she knew what was best for me, and he had agreed. As I'd come down the stairs, ready to go out with Peggy and her friends, and then with dates, he'd smile and tell me I looked beautiful and to have a good time.

He'd give me a quick hug and then stand at the door, watching as we drove away. I knew he loved me. But without my mom, my dad wasn't sure how to raise a daughter.

I pushed memories of what had happened to my mom away; I didn't have time for them yet, promising myself that I would deal with them later. Tonight, it was all about Jack and Bonnie.

What I didn't know at the time was that it was Jack who would bring all those memories back. It was Jack who would fill in details about my mom that I had never known.

If I had known that going out to dinner with the girls would reveal more secrets, some of which I had forgotten on purpose and some of which I had never known, I might not have gone.

Not all the secrets were revealed that night. Just enough to make us all look differently at what we thought we knew. It took time to put the pieces together. And it wasn't me that figured it all out in the end. It was Peggy.

So even though I wanted to know what Harry had told me before walking into the woods that day, when I finally did remember what he had said, it took me a long time to be glad about it.

By the time Peggy pulled into the driveway and honked her horn, I was halfway out the door. It had been a long day, and I was already tired, even though I had that brief nap. But instead of giving into it, I told myself to keep moving. Tonight was about Bonnie, not about me.

Thirty Six

We went somewhere different for dinner. I didn't know that Whispering Pines had so many choices for places to eat. I remembered when all we had was a diner, and everyone went there. Not because the food was good (because it wasn't), but because it was a gathering place.

As we drove, having picked up Bonnie and Faye, Peggy explained why there was more to do in town. It turns out that the internet gave people a chance to live where they wanted to, and many people liked the idea of a small town away from the noise of the city.

And when these newcomers arrived, some of them brought ideas from where they came from and opened small specialty grocery stores and restaurants. This time, as we drove, I saw the town with fresh eyes. This time I saw the improvements and the new trees planted by the curbs.

I looked over at Faye, and she knew what I was thinking.

"You help with some of this," she said.

So I was already helping the town. But that was all Faye. I wanted to be aware of what I was doing. Again, Faye knew what I was thinking: "We'll go over it tomorrow."

Neither Peggy nor Bonnie asked what we were talking about. Either they already knew, decided it was none of their business, or knew we'd eventually tell them about it.

Grace had already arrived and had gotten us a table. She stood to hug everyone, and I thought she looked lovely in a light summer dress and a denim jacket. For a moment, I wished that she would have brought Jenny, but why would she? Jenny hadn't come out with us for a long time, even before Harry died.

For the millionth time, I wondered what I had done so wrong as a mother that Jenny disliked me so much. I knew I hadn't been the best mom ever, but I also knew that even though I had made mistakes, I had always tried to do the right thing.

When Jenny was little, we had so much fun together, but then she started pulling away. I had a little collection of notes from her telling me she hated me. I had put them away, thinking that someday we'd laugh about them together. At the time, I had thought it was a phase she was going through and tried to give her space to go through it while loving her just as much as ever.

If it was a phase, it was a long one. I didn't know if it would make me feel better or worse to hear from her about why she hated me. I shook the thoughts away because here was Grace, who loved me, and my friends, who loved me too. All of them put up with how I had been behaving and understood why. I was the one who didn't understand why.

Dinner was full of chatter, and I loved every minute. As I listened to each of my friends tell about their day, I thought I could feel Harry beside me, listening too. We had spent many times together just like this. Of course, Grace hadn't been there then. Instead, it had been Harry, Faye, Bonnie, Peggy, and me.

Only then did it occur to me that Harry had almost always been the only man at the table. Why was that? Thinking about it, I realized that Bonnie never seemed to have a need for a man in her life. I had never asked her why.

Peggy had been clear about her intentions. When she moved to Whispering Pines to be close to me, she said after three husbands she didn't need another serious relationship. Peggy dated them, but she never allowed them to be part of our groups, saying they didn't fit. She intentionally kept them to herself and then let them drift away. Or she'd push them away. It depended on how one looked at it.

And then there was Faye. Always alone. Except that wasn't true. She was always around Harry and me. Were we the love of her life? And if so, was it both of us or one of us? Or was her life as it was perfect? I thought it was probably that. I had never known Faye to be unhappy or confused about what she wanted.

Grace clinked her water glass with her knife and, lifting it up, said, "Thank you for letting me be a part of the group!"

We all saluted her back, assuring her we loved having her there. It would only be a little longer, and then she'd be off on her own adventures, and we'd be the four grandmothers that she could come home to.

As if she knew what I was thinking, Grace smiled at me and lifted her water glass one more time. I smiled back and then looked down so she wouldn't see the tears in my eyes. I was determined not to spoil her happiness by being sad for myself that she would be gone.

When Harry and I were young, we thought time had expanded forever. Now it felt as if time was collapsing on itself and everything happened at the speed of light. As Grace chatted with Faye, I looked at her, and for a moment, the restaurant faded away, and I saw Grace in the future. It was so real that I gasped, and everyone turned to look at me.

The vision faded. I nodded and said that I was okay, but I swear that Peggy, Faye, and Bonnie looked at me as if they knew what had happened. Was this normal, then? Or is it normal for me? Was this what I had forgotten how to do?

The rest of the meal flew by. I barely registered what I was eating, and then we were up and getting ready for line dancing lessons. Faye helped me with my jacket, and I felt her comforting hand on my shoulder. She knew. I would ask her later what it meant.

But I was ready for a diversion. "I'm ready," I said to her, and I knew she knew what I meant. I wanted to know, but right now, we had Jack and Bonnie to figure out. And that meant everything else had to wait.

Thirty Seven

An hour later, we were all stuffed into a booth at the restaurant next to the bar, not quite as exhausted from the class as we had been the first time. We would have stayed at the bar to talk, but it was just too loud, and of course, that is what we wanted to do. The dancing was fun, but it had been an excuse to get to know Jack better.

It was Grace who convinced Jack to come with us. He was reluctant. Why wouldn't he be? Here we were, four old women, waiting to grill him, and unless he was a dunce, he knew that was going to happen. But Grace said, "Please," and he came.

It wasn't surprising that he had come alone to the line dance lesson, even though you'd think that he would bring Jenny. But I knew Jenny. She would choose to remain home alone, probably lonely, rather than coming out into the world and getting to know people. I suppose we have had that in common for the last eleven years.

I hope I didn't blame other people for my loneliness the way I knew Jenny did. Even as a child, she would choose not to go to birthday parties. I'd force her to go then, and she always seemed to love them once she got there. But then, maybe that was another reason she didn't like me.

Anyway, we dragged Jack out with us, and after he realized it was happening and he couldn't get out of it, he seemed to enjoy himself. Once we had all ordered something and chitchatted about nothing for a moment, Jack looked around the table and asked how we all knew each other.

We all expected Peggy to answer first, but it was Faye who smiled and started us off. She told Jack that she had grown up in Whispering Pines, so she had known both Harry and me when we lived there. Not really known us, knew about us. She was only six when my dad took me away, but she had often seen Harry and me walking in the woods since she had lived only a block away.

Faye told a story about the time Harry and I stopped and talked to her as she stood at the edge of her lawn, wishing she could step into the woods with us. I didn't remember doing that, but she said we had brought her a red trillium flower that we had picked while walking.

"I was just a kid," Faye said. "But it made a huge impression on me. Mabel and Harry were who I wanted to be like. Free in the woods. Even then, it was obvious that they belonged together."

That was a story I had never heard before, and I thanked Faye for telling it.

Faye then explained how she had stayed in Whispering Pines and worked as an assistant to my dad's estate attorney. When the attorney mentioned to Faye that he was trying to locate the daughter of one of his clients who had died, she recognized my name and asked if she could contact me.

Then I took over the story and explained how I had moved away at ten, and Harry had moved away not too many years later. I said that at the time of my father's death, I had been living in downtown Los Angeles, working as a stockbroker. When Faye found me, I was newly divorced and ready for a change. It was Faye who convinced me to come home and live in the house that dad had left me.

"You lived in Los Angeles?" Jack exclaimed. I could see he saw me a little differently now. I expected he had quite a few opinions of me already based on anything Jenny had said.

"I did. And so did Peggy, although she moved away."

"So you knew Peggy in California?"

"We went to high school together. Actually, she was like a big sister to me. She took care of me and made sure I got through school. She saved me from myself, and from the bullying that I experienced until Peggy came along."

Peggy laughed and added that she had found me hiding behind the dumpster in the back of the school and felt sorry for me. But even more than that, she was angry at the kids who were so stupid that they got their kicks out of harassing other kids and wanted to teach them a lesson.

"By taking care of Mabel?" Jack asked. "How is that a lesson to the mean kids?"

Peggy shrugged. But I had seen it work. In her own way, she forced people to be nice. If you wanted to run with the cool crowd, Peggy had to approve, and if you were mean, you were out.

"But how did you end up here?" Jack asked.

Peggy explained that although she had moved away after high school, she kept in touch with me. She had married a few times, had multiple careers, and settled on selling real estate. But when she left her third husband, she moved to Whispering Pines because that was where I lived. She had enough money saved that she didn't need to work anymore, but she kept her real estate license anyway because she just couldn't sit around doing nothing.

That led to a discussion about how she and Jack could work together. Houses always needed to be fixed both before and after a sale. Jack said he was thinking about buying houses to flip them. Maybe they could work that way together, too.

It was all very cozy, and it felt as if we were building a nice little community of people. I couldn't believe I had missed out on all this over the last few years.

Bonnie had been quiet the whole time, but once Peggy finished explaining and planning with Jack, we turned to her to tell her story. Although Bonnie didn't look happy about it, she shared that she had moved to Whispering Pines in her early twenties, got a job teaching, and had been there ever since.

"And that's how we met," I added. "She was one of Jenny's teachers. In fact, more than half of the people in town had Bonnie as a teacher. I think it's because of her we have such kind people living here."

Bonnie blushed and looked down at the table. But as I said it, I realized how true it was. She was sitting beside me, so I gave her a little one-armed hug and then asked the question that we had all been waiting to ask.

"What about you, Jack? Where did you grow up?"

If I hadn't had my arm around Bonnie, I might not have felt her shutter. I squeezed her a little tighter as we waited for the answer.

Thirty Eight

I barely slept that night. All I could think about was what Jack had said. And Bonnie's departure. As he told his story about his life, she excused herself and left the restaurant, saying she'd take an Uber home.

Later, Peggy explained what an Uber was to me, but at the time I was too stunned by Bonnie's leaving to ask. I think everyone was. Bonnie always stayed to the end of everything, always gracious and willing to listen to anyone's story about anything.

Not this time. She claimed she had a headache and had to leave. We offered to leave too, but she refused and was out the door even before we could move. We were all so shocked by what had happened that we all sat there for a few minutes longer, staring at each other.

"Was it something I said?" Jack asked.

We assured him it wasn't, but it appeared that way. Whatever happened, it had stopped the conversations and story-telling. We tried, but our hearts weren't in it. After a few awkward minutes, Jack asked Grace if she needed a ride home. She said sure, having walked to the restaurant. Once the two of them left, it was just the three of us sitting there, wondering how the evening had fallen apart like that.

I went over the story Jack told in my head as I tried to sleep. Jack had explained that he had come to Whispering Pines because his mother had visited it once and told him about it.

When his parents died in a car crash because a drunk driver had crossed into their lane and hit them head-on, it became impossible for him to stay in his hometown. It was a small town, and he would often have to drive past where they had died.

"One day I remembered mom telling me about Whispering Pines, so I came here, fell in love with it, and stayed," he told us.

After telling him how sorry we were about his parents, we asked how he ended up in construction. It turned out that it was his dad who got him interested, and instead of going to college, he had gone to multiple trade schools to learn the skills he had now.

The entire time Jack had been talking, Bonnie had become quieter and quieter. I had thought nothing of it. It was getting late, and we were all used to going to bed early, so I assumed she was just getting tired.

But when Peggy asked Jack to tell more about his parents, and he casually mentioned that they adopted him when he was a newborn and he knew nothing about his birth parents, Bonnie stopped breathing and then said she had to go.

Looking back, it seemed that it was the adoption statement that had been the last straw. So although we assured Jack that it was not something he said that caused Bonnie to leave, it actually appeared that it had been.

Once Jack and Grace left, the three of us left too. Faye asked if we thought Bonnie was okay, and we all shrugged. We had wanted to find out about Jack and help Bonnie. Yes, we had learned more about Jack, but we didn't appear to be helping Bonnie. In fact, we had made it worse.

As before, Peggy dropped me off last. Before I got out of the car, she turned to me and asked me if I was feeling more like myself.

"You mean, am I remembering things? "

"Yes. And anything more than that?"

But even though I was fairly sure she was referring to the visions I was having, I was reluctant to admit anything, so I just shrugged.

Peggy sighed and then asked me to let her know if anything occurred to me about why Bonnie had left so abruptly.

As I lay in bed, I knew what Peggy wanted. Somehow I was supposed to see into the past, or maybe the future, to find out what was happening with Bonnie. And to find out what, if anything, did it have to do with Jack?

But even if I had once known how to consciously produce visions, I didn't remember how to do it now. But now, with Bonnie's happiness at stake, I wanted to, so I lay in bed trying to make something happen. Which made my brain go around and around in circles.

I knew enough to know that was exactly the opposite of how visions occurred. It wasn't by forcing them. Finally, after a few hours of tossing and turning, I drifted off to sleep. One last question floated by, as I did. Where did Bonnie grow up? Did she ever tell us? And what did that have to do with anything, anyway?

The next morning, I tried calling Bonnie. But her phone just rang and rang. Concerned, I called Faye and then Peggy to find out if they knew where she was. Faye was working at the allotments, and Peggy was showing a house to a prospective customer, but they both said not to worry.

But I did. I worried so much that I decided to go to Bonnie's house and see if she was there. It had been ages since I last drove myself somewhere, but once I slid behind the wheel, it all came back to me. When Grace got her driver's license, she had taken the car out once in a while, so I knew it worked.

I drove to Bonnie's, consumed with worry. I had been in that place many times before Harry died. But since then, I couldn't remember feeling this way. Maybe not wanting to be worried was why I shut down.

When I pulled up in front of her house, it looked the same as I remembered. It was a small house that looked like a cottage out of a fairy tale. A weeping cherry tree bloomed on her front lawn. A paved stone sidewalk led to a blue front door set inside a small porch. The porch was just big enough for a wood bench and a pot of tulips that had finished blooming.

It was mid-morning by the time I got to her house, but her curtains were closed. Not like Bonnie at all. I rang the doorbell, but she didn't answer. Walking around to the back of the house, everything seemed in order.

A trellis-covered back patio, where we had often sat and talked, was empty. I pulled a chair up to the garage window, carefully stood on it, and looked in. It was empty.

Stepping off the chair, I sat down on it and called Faye and Peggy again. When I told them Bonnie was gone, they laughed and said she probably went to teach or shop.

But when I told them both that Bonnie's curtains were closed, that changed everything. Bonnie always got up early, and as the sun rose, she opened her curtains. Everyone knew that.

Bonnie greeted the day, ready to help every kid and grown kid in town. And now she wasn't answering her phone. the car was gone, and the curtains were closed.

I knew now that Bonnie was missing, and I was afraid. Bonnie was the glue that held us all together. Why would she go without talking to any of us? And where would she go?

We knew so little about Bonnie's past that I didn't know if she had family somewhere else that she may have gone to visit. What kind of friend had I been that I knew so little about her life?

And now, something had scared her off. But what was it? And where was she?

Thirty Nine

We searched for Bonnie. All of us did. We even got the police involved. But they assured us that since there was no sign of a struggle and because she had hired someone to take care of her house, she had obviously chosen to go somewhere.

Weeks went by, and Bonnie's house stayed empty. Flowers bloomed and died, and Grace went to camp. But we still hadn't found Bonnie.

In her absence, other things we had put into action kept going. Before Grace left for camp, she had set up a checklist for me to follow to get the house repaired. When I told her I was going to sell the house and find someplace else to live, she turned her face away.

When I asked her what was wrong, she sniffed and said nothing, but when I made her look at me, I saw tears running down her cheeks.

It had never occurred to me that she wouldn't want me to sell the house, but since she said she didn't want to talk about it, I had promised her I'd put off the decision until she got back from camp.

So, in the meantime, I continued to make it the best it could be. Following Grace's checklist made it easy, and Jack took care of his end with no prompting on my part. Being so busy with the house helped keep my mind off of not knowing where Bonnie had gone. And why.

We stopped line dancing after Bonnie left. It didn't feel right without her, so I only saw Jack when he came to check on the house construction. Jack and I never talked about that night. I knew he felt guilty that somehow he had caused Bonnie's disappearance, but we all assured him he had done nothing wrong.

And yet it was obvious her disappearance was about Jack. But what? The what kept us all speculating every time we got together. But neither Peggy nor Faye knew more than I did. We just kept praying that Bonnie was okay and would return to us soon.

Pete Woods had done such a beautiful job of clearing out the path into my woods that I had asked him to stay and help me with the backyard. Still thinking I might sell the house, I wanted it to appeal to more people, which meant it needed a lawn of sorts.

There wasn't much of one in the front and just weeds in the back. In the front yard, an enormous maple tree took up one half of the space between the house and the sidewalk. I had always left one side free of trees so that I could see the house across the street. But that piece of lawn was in sad shape.

Pete came up with a plan to put a garden box or two on the side of the patio in the back, after he fixed the patio, and the rest would be lawn with a stone path that led from the patio and back door to the path in the woods.

He would use the same stone as the patio and curve it so it would be more appealing. Then he would update the lawn and plants in the front yard.

The more Pete stayed around, the more I liked him. In some ways, he reminded me of Harry. Quiet and hard working. But in other ways, they were quite different. Harry would work in his office, and then be gone for weeks at a time. Pete worked where I could see him, and when I quizzed him a little about his life, I found out he had never left Whispering Pines.

Often in the middle of the day, I'd invite Pete for a chat on the patio. I'd bring lemonade and cookies and he'd take a break from his work, washing his hands with the hose, and drying them on a towel he kept in his truck. He said he didn't want to come inside with his dirty clothes on, which I appreciated.

In one of our chats, Pete told me about his wife who had died a few years before. Like Harry and me, they had known each other since childhood. They had become high school sweethearts. She had gone off to college, but came home afterward, and they had married.

What I didn't tell Pete was that I had seen his wife all along. As Pete talked about her, she was standing behind him, smiling. By then I had gotten used to having visions, if there was such a thing as getting used to seeing things that weren't really there. But at least I didn't panic when they happened.

I watched her as she watched him. She smiled at me and I couldn't help but smile back.

"It's a lovely story," I said to Pete, watching his wife Louise. "What did she look like?"

As Pete described her, the way she looked when they were young, and then before she died, he was describing the women standing behind his chair.

I had long ago accepted that nobody ever dies. After all, I saw them. Not the material person. Something else. Not a ghost either. I thought of it as their essence, visible enough for me to see it. I had to accept that the essence of who we are continues forever, but they didn't always stay around for us to see them. There were many other places for them to be.

I knew enough physics to know that matter is an illusion, something about waves and particles, and that the energy of who we are remains like radio waves. Or at least that is how someone described it, and that made sense to me.

When Pete saw me smiling, he asked me why. I didn't tell him that his wife, Louise, was standing behind him. I wasn't sure how he would take it. Instead, I said that she was probably watching over him the same way that Harry watched over me.

Pete smiled then, put down his lemonade and said, "I know that must be true. Sometimes I feel her with me as if she is right beside me."

"I bet she is, Pete," I said, and smiled again at Louise. She smiled and winked back at me.

Gathering up the lemonade and plates, I went back into the house to read. I was deep into one of Harry's books when Pete called out to me through the screen door. He was working in the lilac bush. Now that it had finished blooming, he was trimming out the dead wood.

When I came to the door, he held something up, and asked, "What's this?"

As I stepped outside to look, the vision hit me so hard I almost fell over. If Pete hadn't been there, I might have. He helped me to the chair. I closed my eyes, and I was back to the day that Harry and I had planted the lilac.

Forty

I'm not sure what I looked like to Pete, but it must have scared him, because he picked up my phone that I had left on the patio table and found Faye's and Peggy's numbers and called them.

I didn't see him do it. I had my head in my arms on the table. It was as if I was in two places, or two times, at once. Same back yard, same patio, same table, but in one place and time there was Pete calling my friends, and in the other it was Harry and me planting the lilac bush.

On that long-ago day, the sky was a brilliant shade of spring blue, and a gentle breeze carried the fresh, earthy scent of newly turned soil. Harry and I, armed with shovels and youthful enthusiasm, had chosen the perfect spot for the lilac bush, envisioning how it would grow and bloom beside the back door, so its fragrance could drift into the house.

We laughed and joked as we dug. The physical labor was a shared endeavor, a celebration of sharing our lives together in that house. And the lilac bush was a symbol of how we felt about each other.

We had Jenny, and I was making friends. Faye had always been there, but we had Bonnie and Peggy, which helped when Harry had to travel.

Half way through digging the hole, Harry suddenly became serious, his playfulness gone. I remember it had scared me a little. Harry was often intense when he was writing, but rarely at other times. He took my hand, covered in dirt and sweat, and held it tightly.

"Mabel," he said, his eyes locking on mine with a seriousness that took my breath away. "This lilac bush—it's more than just a plant. It's a symbol of us, of our roots in this place, and of the growth we're yet to experience."

I remember feeling a surge of emotion—a mix of joy, anticipation, and a hint of fear. I already knew what he was telling me. Why tell me again so seriously? The moment was charged with an unspoken question. Did he know something about our future that he was afraid to tell me?

But before I could respond, before I could ask him to explain, we were interrupted. A neighbor called out with a trivial question about borrowing a garden tool. After speaking to our neighbor, we returned to our task, but the intensity of the moment was gone. However, the memory of that moment, the seriousness in Harry's voice, and the look in his eyes, stayed with me.

Now, years later, as Pete held up the object he found buried near the roots of the mature lilac bush, the memory crashed over me as real as the day we had planted the bush.

It was a small, rusted metal box, unmistakably the one Harry had mysteriously brought with him that day. He had insisted on placing it beneath the bush before we filled the hole, claiming it was a tradition to ensure the plant's vitality.

I had forgotten about the box until now, its significance lost in the tides of time and the layers of life lived since that day. But here it was, a tangible link to the past, to Harry, and to the unanswered questions that day had left in my heart.

With trembling hands, I opened the box, Pete watching silently, respectfully, giving me space to confront whatever secrets it held. Inside, wrapped in a now-faded piece of cloth, was a key and a note in Harry's handwriting, aged but legible, addressed to me.

"Mabel," it read, "if you're reading this, then the time is right. The key unlocks a truth I couldn't share—something I learned. I hope you can forgive my silence. However, I know you like a little mystery, so I hope you will enjoy discovering what this key opens. Know that my love for you is as enduring as the lilac we planted together."

Tears blurred my vision as I clutched the note, the weight of Harry's words anchoring me to the spot. What truth had he hidden? What had he been unable to share? And how had he kept this from me for all those years?

I looked up at Pete, a silent plea in my eyes. I needed to find out what the key was. I needed to uncover Harry's secret to understand the man I loved and the legacy he left behind.

Is this why Harry was still hanging around? And then a strange thought occurred to me. Did it have something to do with Bonnie and why she was missing? But how could that be? How could these things possibly be related?

By the time Faye and Peggy arrived, I had returned to just one time and place. The vision had faded, but not my confusion.

I thanked Pete for taking care of me, and he suggested that was enough for the day. He nodded, and I saw Louise walking with him as he picked up his tools and headed around the house to his truck.

She turned and looked at me, smiled, and waved. I didn't have the energy to return the wave; I just nodded and did my best to smile.

"Who do you see?" Peggy asked.

When I looked at her, puzzled by what she meant, she and Faye just shook their heads at me.

"We know you see people who have died," Faye answered. "It's good that you are doing it again and not hiding from it."

I cursed before answering, "Pete's wife."

"Why are you mad about it?" Peggy asked with her hands on her hips.

Today she wore a brilliant orange pants suit with a purple belt, and with the sun behind her, it was as if she were on fire. It was impossible not to smile at her. She looked like a huge bird of paradise.

"Why didn't you tell me you knew about me seeing visions?"

Faye took my hand and said, "We did. You just forgot."

I cursed again. I was tired. And now I had a stupid box with a key and a stupid note from Harry.

I handed it all to Faye and said, "Well, what do you know about this?"

Forty One

The next day, I didn't bother to get up. I assured myself that no one would know. I even told myself that no one would care. That part I knew was a lie, but it didn't matter anyway. I wanted to believe that no one would care, because I decided I didn't.

Faye and Peggy claimed they knew nothing about the box, the key, or the note. I had convinced them I needed nothing from them, and they left, but not before reminding me to call if I thought of anything I wanted.

Jay and Dove came to the kitchen door later that afternoon, both of them cawing away at me. I ignored them. I even shut the door on them, something I had never done before. At first, they didn't give up. They tapped on my window for a long time and then finally flew away.

Just like Harry. Harry, who had flown away. Harry, who had always seemed not to be completely present in the world, had finally left to go to another one. Without me. And with a secret that he was afraid to tell me about.

That's all I could think about as I dragged myself up to bed. I didn't lay out clothes, a lifetime habit ignored. I left my clothes on the floor, unheard of for me, pulled on my nightgown, and went to bed.

At first, I slept, exhaustion taking over. But then, a few hours later, I was wide awake, and for the rest of the night, I woke, slept, dreamed, woke, slept, and dreamed until the crack of lightning and the rumble of thunder woke me up for good.

It woke me up but didn't get me up. I had left the curtains open, too not caring to shut them, which meant that I could see the dark sky with the flash of light. I lay there as the sun rose enough that I could see the dark clouds and rain running down the window, and I felt massively sorry for myself.

Everyone had left me. Grace was at camp, would soon go away to college, and probably would never speak to me again. Why would she? I was just her old grandmother. Her world was wide open with possibilities. Mine had closed down.

My daughter had stopped speaking to me years before, so she had left me. Even before finally leaving me for good, Harry had often left me as he traveled. And although he was diligent about checking in, he was gone anyway, leaving me alone in this house. And now he was gone forever.

Then there was Bonnie. She got up and left me, too. It didn't matter that she had left everyone. What mattered was me. She had left me.

It didn't matter that Faye and Peggy had gone nowhere, because I knew for sure that soon they would leave me, too. Friends die all the time. And now, the older I got, more friends die more often.

I'd see their name in the newspaper and the list of people they left behind, and I'd wonder what would happen if they listed all the people each of us leave behind. Wouldn't it be hundreds, if not more? They left this world and the ones who loved them behind. That's what Harry had done.

It always came back to that. Harry had left me behind, going where I could not follow. And even if I did, would he be there?

Wherever he was, was that the world he had been yearning for his whole life? The one without me in it?

Yes, part of me knew I was exaggerating about all of it. Making it more of a tragedy than it actually was. But did I care? I did not.

So I lay in bed and cried, slept, and didn't get up. Even when the phone rang, I lay there. Even when Jay flew to the window of my bedroom and tapped at me to get up, I lay there.

I'd had enough. And because it was raining, I didn't have to call anyone and tell them not to come over. The construction crew would stay home. And I would stay in bed.

The day grew darker as the storm increased, matching my mood exactly.

And then Faye was there by my bed, shaking me and saying, "Get up." Sunshine was streaming through the window. The storm was over. I wasn't happy about that.

I moaned and rolled over.

She didn't say anything else, but I could hear her pick up my clothes off the floor and then the clinking of dishes downstairs.

Soon I smelled coffee brewing, and despite myself, I started getting hungry.

Cursing all the good people in the world, the ones who insist that we keep on living even when we don't want to, and love you even when you are an angry old woman. I pulled the covers up over my head.

But it was useless. I was hungry. I wanted coffee. I had to pee.

Life was relentless. Even when I didn't want to live it, it just kept going, as if my feelings didn't matter.

Forty Two

When Faye came back upstairs with a mug of coffee and said, "Sit up," I obeyed. She propped pillows up behind me and waited for me to say something.

I pointed at the bathroom, not willing to speak to anyone just yet, and she helped me up so I could go. When I returned to the bedroom, she helped me back to bed, fluffed the pillows, and handed me the coffee.

Settling in the chair by the bed, the one where Harry would sometimes sit to read when he couldn't sleep, she sipped her cup of tea and waited.

I knew Faye well enough to know that she would wait me out. But I didn't care. I wasn't talking. Even though I knew I'd have to eventually give in, it wasn't right at the moment. I was prepared to milk my pity party for as long as it took to get what I wanted. Whatever that was.

We drank in silence. I was mad that I was feeling better. I wanted to lie back down in bed and never get up. I wanted to not care, so I could drift away and maybe go where Harry went. I wanted people to feel upset with themselves because they hadn't loved me enough.

When I heard that last thought in my head, it stopped everything. *What did that mean? How long have I been thinking about things like that?* And despite my lingering desire to give up, I realized it would not happen just because I wanted it to. Life would not be depositing me on some other shore just yet.

So since I had to keep living, what was I going to do about all the things I was mad or sad about, depending on the moment? I put my coffee on the side table, sighed, leaned back into the pillows, closed my eyes, and let the tears fall.

Faye waited, still not saying anything. I felt no pity or even compassion coming from her. She was simply there, waiting for me to decide what I wanted to do. I knew she had already decided she'd be there for me, no matter what.

How she knew to do that and put away her ego and the thoughts that get in the way, I don't know. As I slowly decided that I could live with my sorrow, fear, and anger, even if they never went away, I realized that I hardly knew Faye at all.

I also realized that she knew how to do something that I apparently didn't. She knew how to simply love without judgement or expectations. And she was my friend. So I must be worth something for her to waste her time on me.

Although I hadn't moved, and the tears still flowed, Faye knew I was ready. I had decided to keep on living. To keep on caring. She stood up and said she'd meet me downstairs.

I was too tired to curse, too tired to complain, and even too tired to dress. But I knew that I wasn't tired enough to die yet, so I had to keep on living, which meant I had to get downstairs.

I left my coffee because I knew Faye would have another cup for me, and carrying it downstairs would be too dangerous. Which is how I knew, once again, that I wasn't ready to fall and break my neck yet. Not ever, actually. That seemed like a cruel way to die, and I didn't want it to be that way.

Smiling to myself and acknowledging that I had some fight left in me, I slipped on my robe and headed downstairs, cursing the whole way. Some things hadn't changed. I think I was happy about that.

Not everyone liked my cursing, which is why it was mostly silent under my breath. But everyone knew I did it. Harry had asked me to stop more than once, and I tried. But I couldn't. Probably because I didn't want to. It was part of me—an outlet that didn't hurt anyone. At least that's what I told myself.

All I could do was not curse out loud as much, and I got very good at the silent mutterings. Harry eventually gave up asking me to stop. I suppose he accepted that if he wanted me, he got cursing. It was a compromise of sorts. Maybe when he was away, he even missed it. Who knows? I never asked.

I found Faye in the kitchen. The note, the key, and the box sat on the tree table. Mocking me. And that made me mad.

When I cursed at them, Faye smiled, handed me another cup of coffee, and said, "Shall we figure this out together?"

"As you wish," I replied.

She laughed, and then I laughed too, surprising myself. The line from "Princess Bride" was simply another way to say, "I love you," and we both knew that was what I meant.

Not for the first time I thought how lucky I was to have friends, and Harry, who accepted me as I was and with whom I had shortcuts and ways of talking that said everything without too many words.

"I love you, too," Faye said, sitting down with her tea at the table.

Unlike Peggy and her loud and crazy clothes, Faye was always in muted colors, like in the twilight part of the day. Even when Faye was still, she seemed to flow. Like flowers in the garden that always seem to move, even when there isn't a breeze.

Today, her dark gray hair flowed down her back over an almost purple tunic she wore over gray yoga pants. As always, she looked soft and gentle, but I knew underneath she had a strong and unrelenting heart.

Smiling at me, she pulled her computer out of her bag, and I was reminded that she also had a mind that was curious, relentless, and very organized.

We would figure out the puzzle together. I was sure of it.

When she turned to me, I knew what she wanted. She wanted me to say out loud what I had been thinking.

"For some reason, I think this note has something to do with why Bonnie is missing."

Leaning forward, her dark blue eyes looking at me as if she could see everything, she asked, "And what leads you to think that?"

If I had ever wanted a vision to give me an answer, it was then, but nothing happened.

I shook my head. Faye smiled, patted my hand, and turned to her computer. "Well, let's see what we can find out about our friend Bonnie."

Without thinking, I added, "And my mother's death."

Faye didn't blink and didn't show surprise, even though that request surprised me. What did my mother's death have to do with Bonnie, the key, and the note?

Forty Three

Jack chose that moment to show up just ahead of the construction crew. He said that although it was wet outside, they could work inside the house until it dried up more outside.

That news didn't make me happy. People would invade my privacy. But it was my fault that I had invited them. In fact, I was paying them to make a mess of my house. What had I been thinking?

If it surprised Jack to see me in a robe, he didn't show it. Instead, he accepted Faye's offer of a cup of coffee and sat at the table with us.

"Can I help with that?" He asked, gesturing to the tin box. I realized Pete must have told him about it, and then sent Jack over to check on me.

At first, I was offended and then mentally slapped myself for being so stupid. If I wasn't already embarrassed by the way I looked, I might have cursed out loud.

Of course, it was Faye who answered him, saying that we could use all the help we could get, and if he knew what kind of lock the key fit in, that would be extremely helpful.

After turning it over in his hands, he said he didn't, but there were some people on another construction crew who might know. They'd been around longer than him and since the key was old, it might be something they recognized.

It was a polite way of saying we were old, but what else could he do? We were. He promised to take good care of it and return it promptly. I nodded, and Faye put it in a plastic bag, which he zipped into an inner pocket of his jacket.

Excusing myself, I went upstairs to change before the crew arrived. I could hear Faye and Jack talking downstairs, but I couldn't make out what they were saying.

Since it was Faye who was making sure the crew got paid, I assumed that was what they were discussing.

But when I returned, dressed and with my hair combed, feeling marginally better, Faye said she was asking about Jack's parents. Jack nodded at me, genuinely happy to see me feeling better, and I realized he was a nice man. Jenny was a lucky woman. I was happy for her.

Taking a sip of coffee, Jack continued his story. "Mom and dad were the best parents anyone could ask for. If anything, I suppose they were a little overly protective, especially mom.

"Once when I was a teenager and mad about her rules, dad told me that something had happened when she was a teenager that had changed her life, and she didn't want that to happen to me.

"At the time, she didn't tell me what it was. But I found out after they died."

Seeing that we were both caught up in his story, Jack continued. He told us that as he cleaned out his parents' house, he found his mother's journal.

He was fairly sure she didn't mean for anyone to see it because she had burned all her journals one day, saying that she didn't want him to feel responsible for her feelings after she died.

"But she must have missed that one because it was buried deep in a box along with what looked like her cheer leading uniform from high school.

"After reading it, I understood why we never had alcohol in our house, and she was so strict about me and drinking. She was always asking if my friends drank. Always reminding me to think for myself and say no. It really made me mad at the time.

"But after reading her journal, I understood. And the fact that later they were both killed by a drunk driver made their death even worse for me. It took me a long time to get over it."

Taking another sip of his coffee, he added. "I never got over it, really. I have just learned to live with it. Sometimes."

We both waited, hoping he'd say more. When he didn't, Faye asked, "Why? What did your mother's journal say?"

"It wasn't specific. It was just pages and pages of grief over a car accident that she was in with a bunch of kids. They were all drunk, and they killed someone. She wasn't driving, but I don't think that made any difference to her."

Just at that moment, there was a loud clap of thunder, and the sky darkened. The storm had returned.

"Well, I guess we'll just be working inside today," Jack said, laughing and breaking the mood. "Mabel, you might not be comfortable with all of us around. Maybe you want to go somewhere."

Faye and I agreed. We called Peggy to see if she wanted to meet us for breakfast. By the time the crew arrived, we were ready to go. I put the note back in the box and put it in the cupboard with the cereal.

What Jack said had started me thinking. We had something in common. My mother had died because of a drunk driver. His parents had died the same way. But what about when his mom was a teenager? What had happened? Who had died? And once again, for some reason, it made me think of Bonnie.

What had Jack said that upset her? Where was she? It was time for the three of us to do some serious searching. I had a lot of questions. What was it about Jack's mother that worried me? What were the details surround my mother's death? Where was Bonnie? What did that key unlock, and what did Harry mean by that note?

I knew Grace would be home in a few days. I wanted some answers by then. And finally, I added the question I had been afraid to ask for too many years because I was afraid of the answer.

Why wouldn't Jenny speak to me? Maybe I couldn't fix it, but at least I wanted to know. I needed to know.

My old list paled compared to this list, but I realized I wouldn't have gotten this far if I hadn't started with the first one. So now I had two lists, or maybe just one that had gotten very long.

I was determined to cross something off it, but first I wanted food.

Forty Four

We met Peggy at the Pancake House. I knew there were many places in other cities and towns with that name, but I am sure none of them are as wonderful as ours.

I giggled to myself when I remembered that when I was little and first heard the name Pancake House, I thought we were going to a house made of pancakes. I still do that sometimes. I see a word or name and think it means something entirely different.

Our Pancake House has been in Whispering Pines for as long as I can remember. Before mom died, we went there every Sunday morning. Somebody had to be really sick for us not to go.

Sometimes it seemed as if the whole town would be there, before church, after church, sometimes both times. The food, the atmosphere, everything about it was that good. You could have breakfast or lunch at any time. The staff was quick and friendly, and no one rushed you to leave.

There was always a long line to get in, but it moved quickly. Besides, no one minded, (except maybe somebody from out of town who didn't understand why we didn't mind standing in line). It gave everyone a chance to catch up on gossip or discuss something. Who needed phones when you could see everyone at least once a week?

Standing in line at the Pancake House was as much a meeting place as the church. People hugged, whispered, and mingled. It didn't matter if you stepped out of line to talk to someone; everyone knew where your place in line was when you were done.

The line outside the restaurant is where all the talking goes on, because once inside—although someone would often stop by your table to say hello—it is all about eating.

There was a line this time too, not as long as the Sunday line, but long enough for Peggy to say hello to every person in it. There is an awning that covers the front of the restaurant that people at the front of the line could stand under to stay dry. Everyone else huddled under umbrellas.

It wasn't raining hard, and it was warm, so no one was complaining. Maybe it was the smell of warm pancakes that drifted out of the building that kept us all in such good moods.

While we waited, I saw a woman and her daughter huddling under an umbrella, with a man standing beside them. It took me a minute to realize that no one else saw him and that he and his family were all crying.

My heart broke for them, and I asked Peggy who they were.

Instead of answering, she said, "Is he with them?"

When I nodded yes, she told me to go tell them.

"What? Just walk over and tell them?"

"Mabel, it's what people know you do. Go tell them."

As I approached them, the mom and daughter looked up at me, and I realized Peggy was right. They knew why I was coming over to talk to them and were happy to see me. How could I have missed out on this? What was I thinking? That I was the only one who had lost someone, and that made me more important?

I stood with them for a few minutes. He told them what he wanted them to know: that he'd be nearby for a while, but then he'd go elsewhere, but that they would meet again. The three of us stood and hugged as they thanked me. And the man put his arm around all of us as he, too, thanked me.

All my sadness and anger melted away. Everything in life wasn't all about me. I had fallen for a lie about life and succumbed to the temptation to make life about me and my feelings. For a moment, it felt like a mist, or vale, lifted, and I could clearly see the oneness of life and each of our places in it.

The vision lasted less than a second, but the feeling of lightness and of letting go remained. I felt years younger. Although it was still raining, it felt as if the sun had come out.

I couldn't believe that all of that joy happened simply because I had done something for someone else without thinking about what I would get from it. Was life this easy? I thought it might be.

As I walked back to Faye and Peggy, who were just going through the door, I realized I hadn't seen Harry for a while. I wondered if it was because he was sure I was okay—was I?—or because he didn't want to be around when I found out what the key would open.

I assumed it was the latter.

As we waited for our food, which I knew wouldn't take long, I pulled the little notebook out of my purse where I had written my old list. First, I crossed out things I had been doing, and then I added the new list.

When I was done, I shared it with Faye and Peggy, asking if I had missed anything. Peggy added, *Bring Bonnie home,* and then the food arrived, and it was all about warm blueberry pancakes with real maple syrup.

The entire restaurant was filled with happy people, including me. I resolved to resist giving in to my poor self-pitying thoughts since I knew I would eventually find the answers I sought. Even though I knew I would sometimes lose the battle, I also knew I had decided that it wouldn't keep me down.

We would find the answers. I knew Bonnie was counting on us to do so, that many of these questions revolved around her, and although I didn't know how or why, we would find out, and then she could come home.

I pulled out my lists, intending to share it with Faye and Peggy. But first I reviewed it and crossed out things I either finished or was actively working on. I did it because I liked the feeling of crossing things off, but also to refocus on what was important.

Then I put it on the table for Faye and Peggy to see and held my breath, worried about what they would say.

Old List:

- ~~Do something to help the town.~~

- ~~Clean up my garden. Clear the paths in the woods.~~

- ~~Talk to people.~~

- Help Bonnie.

- Find out more about Faye, Bonnie, and Peggy's lives.

- ~~Fix the bird feeders and get bird food.~~

- ~~Fix the house.~~

- Sell the house and find a place to live.

- ~~Get stronger.~~

New List: Get answers to these questions.

- How did my mother die? Where was she when it

happened? Why did it happen?

- Why doesn't Jenny speak to me?

- Why did Bonnie leave?

- Where is Bonnie now?

- Bring Bonnie home.

- What about Jack's adoptive and real mother?

- What does the key fit?

- What had Harry known, and why was he afraid to tell me?

- What did Harry tell me before he died I couldn't remember?

Forty Five

I didn't need to worry. They loved the lists. They congratulated me on all the crossed-out items on the first list and agreed to help me complete every item on both lists. The question was, what did I want to deal with first?

I stared at the lists, thinking that they were all important, but what I yearned to know first was who was responsible for my mother's death. Yes, I knew she had been killed because a drunk driver ran a red light. But who was it? And where was it? Exactly what happened and why?

Until that moment, I hadn't thought about why I didn't know the answer to any of those questions. Of course, dad had avoided telling me the details when I was ten, but after that, I didn't ask him about it either.

Perhaps I had asked and dad had avoided the answers, but more likely it was because after her death everything changed and that was hard enough to deal with. My mother was gone, and that was that. I had let her go because I couldn't stand the thought that she wasn't there anymore. I hadn't even known where she was buried until I buried my dad beside her.

All those thoughts of what I could have done and should have done tried to pull me back into feeling sorry for myself again, but I chose not to let them. What good would letting them have any power do? If anything, they would be another excuse for giving up. I was tired of that. So I said no to the self-blame that was trying to smother my new life.

Glancing at my lists one more time before I put them back in my purse, I promised myself I would get the things on my lists completed before I died. And since I had recently been hoping that would be soon, I apologized to whatever God was listening and said I didn't mean it. I had stuff to do first.

Peggy volunteered to do the search for information about my mom. She made her own list and said she'd find out and let us know. Of course, I could have done it myself, but I knew what Peggy was doing. She was putting a buffer between me and the answer. Just as my father had done. He never wanted to talk about it. Ever.

But I trusted Peggy would look it up and then tell me in a way that might not break my heart all over again.

Since Jack was looking into where the key might belong and Peggy was looking into the Bonnie and Mom questions, and as hard as I tried, I couldn't get myself to remember what Harry had told me, that left only a few things left on the list for me to do for now.

I had to find a new place to live and talk to Jenny. Since Peggy would be the one helping me sell the house and find another one, that left only one thing: talking to Jenny.

That terrified me more than anything else on the list. I had avoided the question and the answer I was afraid I'd get for years. If Jenny and I happened to see each other, we'd both be polite. But we rarely did. She had avoided me like the plague for years.

Once again, Faye waited for me to acknowledge what was next. She didn't even need an explanation of what I meant when I said, "But how will I do it?"

Instead of answering that question, she asked, "When did it start?"

I knew what she meant by the question. When did Jenny start not talking to me? Was it gradual, or did it happen all at once? What had I missed?

For the next hour, I avoided the issue of talking to Jenny and talked about her instead. Although Faye had been there the whole time, I told her what I remembered as if she hadn't been.

I told her how Jenny and I used to shop together and how much fun that had been. Even when Jenny was little, we would often pull out the same outfit at the same time and then dissolve in laughter over it.

And how, after recognizing Jenny's artistic talent, I turned over all holiday decorations to her, even though, at the time, I had loved doing it myself. I talked about how much I loved shopping for Jenny for her birthday and Christmas.

Everything about Jenny growing up delighted me. In my memory, we had many delightful times together. Yes, she had often been mad at me. She didn't like my rules, but I believed that helping her form good habits that would serve her the rest of her life was part of being a good parent, and she'd grow out of it.

I told Faye about the times Jenny would give me the evil eye when I said something, as if I had somehow switched on something inside her that made her mad at me.

I knew she didn't like her name, Jenny, and she often complained about it. She only really accepted her name when I told her that it was her father who named her, not me.

For Jenny, Harry could do no wrong. Although she would go through spells where she was mad at me, she was never mad at Harry.

In some ways, it didn't seem fair. I was always the one there for her. I was the one who cried for her at night when I knew she was unhappy. I loved having her as my daughter. But she only loved having me as her mother some of the time.

The change was gradual at first. It seemed she was mad at me more often than sharing fun times together. I knew she didn't like my rules, but they weren't harsh; they were just guidelines. I knew I wasn't the perfect mother. I had my own bad days.

Even though at first I tried to talk about what pulled us apart, eventually I gave up. And then one day, the daughter I knew and loved was not there anymore. The one who loved talking and shopping with me was gone.

Instead, there was a semi-polite and then belligerent teenager. And when she went off to college, and when she returned, pregnant, she stopped talking to me all together. She refused all help from me. When Grace was born she put up with my fusing over her, but mainly because I would be with Harry.

So, the answer to Faye's question as to when it started was that it was gradual until after she returned from college.

"Well, maybe the answer is to dial it back in the same way. Gradually include her in some way. And perhaps Jack could help with that. Then, over time, she'll be comfortable talking to you about why she has withdrawn. Maybe she is looking for a way back the same way you are."

The thought that it might be true took my breath away. The idea that I might get my daughter back, even in some small way, made me want to cry. I didn't, though. After all, we were still at the Pancake House.

Trying not to cry at the Pancake House made me think of the mother and daughter I had seen earlier. I looked around the restaurant and saw them tucked back against the wall. No longer crying. Consciously, or unconsciously, they had left room for the man. And there he was, smiling at them and then at me.

Yes, that is what I would do. Make room for Jenny, in whatever form she wants to appear in my life.

"And I have the perfect place to start," Faye said. "Your birthday."

I stared at her as if she had two heads. First, I had forgotten I had a birthday coming up, and second, I never celebrated them.

For good reason. It was the same day that Mom died.

Forty Six

"Absolutely not," I told Faye. I said, "No, no, and no," again. I shouldn't have bothered. Faye just waited out my temper tantrum.

We had left the Pancake House and gone to Faye's. I had waited to say no until we were in the car, and I said it all the way to her house. Faye just drove, smiling to herself. Very annoying.

However, once we got to her house, it was hard to stay mad or upset. Stepping into Faye's world was like being transported to another time and place. It was almost as if we drove through a bubble, and then there was her house and garden, looking exactly like what a fairy house and garden might look like.

It had been a long time since I had been to Faye's house. She always came to mine. Perhaps she liked her privacy even more than I protected mine. But when she brought me again to her magical place, it filled me with happiness, and all my upset disappeared again.

Still not saying anything, Faye made us tea, took a few cookies from a tin—ones I knew she made herself—and let me go to her back garden.

It wasn't as if Faye had a big house or lots of land. In fact, it was tiny. It just felt enormous, as if it existed in another universe. Her backyard was an entirely walled-in garden filled with flowers of all kinds. A small apple tree took up one corner, and evergreens ran across the front of the side wall, filled with singing birds going in and out of the branches.

The rain had stopped again, and the sun was making every drop of water shine like diamonds. I watched as birds flew to the water bath, to the food, and back into the trees. Three robins splashed in the birdbath, and a squirrel sat beneath it, waiting his turn.

Although there wasn't any music playing, it felt as if in Faye's garden there was a symphony of harmony going on.

Tears filled my eyes. This time, the tears were for the beauty of it all and my gratitude that Faye was my friend. She had always felt as if she came from a different place, but in her house and garden, I was sure of it.

Seeing I was ready, Faye said. "Yes, a birthday party. To celebrate life. A small gathering. And if you wish, we could have it here."

I swear that as I thought of what Faye was suggesting, I heard and felt the heavens humming. How could I say no? My birthday was less than a week away. So instead of resisting, I started talking about all the things I needed to do to prepare, but Faye shushed me.

She said she would take care of it all. Grace would be home in a few days, and she'd help, and she'd get her mother to the party. As Faye reminded me, I had other things to think about.

Faye said we'd use the party to not only celebrate my life but my mother's, too. It was time to deal with the pain of losing her. After all, I knew people didn't actually die. They moved on. Perhaps my mother moved on to where I couldn't see her, done with the world. Or perhaps I had never seen her again because I was afraid to.

As Faye talked about the party, I realized I was quite excited about it. Perhaps it would be a new beginning for Jenny and me.

Besides, Faye assured me that by then we would know the complete story about my mother's death, have found Bonnie, and brought her home.

I decided to believe Faye. Why not? Not believing her would certainly never help. But I also knew things didn't happen just by wishing they would; I needed to do some things myself.

And one of them was talking to Jack. I needed to know more about his life. Especially if he was planning on spending more of it with my daughter. Yes, she was a grown woman, but I was her mother, and I was determined to act like it again.

Faye didn't live that far from me, so I walked home, hoping that Jack would still be there. I was relieved to see his truck still in my driveway, and I could hear pounding inside the house. Two more trucks were parked along the curb, so I knew some carpenters would still be there, too.

Jack saw me coming and held open the door, saying that I had arrived at the perfect time. He had just finished inside, and he wanted to talk to me about something.

After showing me what they had fixed, among them the shaky banister, Jack and I sat in the living room. He sat in Harry's chair, and for a minute I was upset. I then reminded myself that it was possible that Jack would be the new head of the family someday. Things changed.

"After we're done with all the repairs, do you want us to paint the inside and outside of the house?"

I thought about how much nicer it would look then and said, "Yes, that's a good idea. That would make it worth more, anyway."

"You're thinking of selling?" Jack asked. "Why? This is such a beautiful home."

When I told him I was worried about going up and down the stairs and that the house was too big for one person, he leaned back and closed his eyes. A few moments later, he said he had an idea.

"Why not turn your dining room, which you never use, into your bedroom? We could connect it to the downstairs bathroom to make you a private suite."

"But what about upstairs? What use would it be?"

"Perhaps a room for Grace? She's talked about moving out and finding her own place. Jenny's house is cramped with the three of us in it."

Until then, I hadn't realized that Jack actually lived with Jenny. But I kept my surprise to myself and said I'd think about it. I also told him about the party Faye was planning and I hoped he and Jenny would come to it.

He knew what I was asking. I wanted him to smooth my way back into Jenny's life. He smiled and said he'd make sure they were there, and I thought my heart would burst wide open.

As he prepared to leave, I asked Jack if he had any friends where he came from that he'd like to have come to the party. He said no. When his parents died, there was nothing left for him in Spring Falls.

Later, as I was staring at the dining room and thinking about what Jack had said about changing it into a bedroom, I wondered where I had heard the name Spring Falls. Had Jack mentioned it before? I didn't think so, but it sounded familiar.

Like so many things these days, the memory sat back in my mind, like a partially open door. I just had to wait for the door to open the entire way for me to remember why I knew the name.

However, I almost didn't want to remember, because just thinking about it made me upset. Which meant Spring Falls wasn't associated with anything happy for me.

I silently cursed, and then I cursed out loud; there was no one to hear me. Why not? For a moment, I felt marginally better.

Forty Seven

The answer as to why I knew the name Spring Falls came to me a few days later. Not because I remembered on my own. Peggy told me. And then I remembered.

Peggy, who had taken her assignment to find Bonnie seriously, had practically disappeared for days. I didn't hear from her at all. Faye did, but whatever Peggy said to Faye, she didn't share with me. I knew they were waiting to tell me face-to-face.

In the meantime, Faye, ever the guardian of our collective spirit, prepared for the birthday celebration with a fervor that spoke volumes of her affection and care for everyone involved.

Faye told Peggy about the party, and I knew that it had made her even more determined to have all the answers as soon as possible. She said it helped to know that my mother had died on my birthday, something I had told no one before. It was just too terrible to share.

With Peggy, Bonnie, and Grace gone and Faye working on the birthday party, that left me with nothing to do but learn more about Jack and his parents.

Grace helped with that. She had come home from working at the camp tanned and happy. Not having seen her for weeks, I had kept a picture of her in my head, and when she returned, it surprised me how wrong that picture had been.

I didn't want to admit it, but I could finally see that Grace wasn't a teenager anymore. Not really. Instead, she had grown into a beautiful young woman. And even though I was grateful to have her home, I knew once she went off to college, everything would change.

I realized what Jack had suggested could work in my favor. If Grace liked the idea, it would mean I might have a chance of keeping her around me for a few more years. My house would be the one she returned to during college. Who knew what would happen after that? Would I even be around then, anyway?

Grace had picked up croissants and coffee from her favorite cafe. It was a chilly morning, so we ate in the kitchen at the tree table. After pulling apart my croissant—it always seemed to taste better that way—and taking a sip of coffee, I told her I had something to ask her.

As I gathered my thoughts, I traced the circles of the tree table, something I found always helped me. It was as if the tree was giving me strength, saying to me, "Look how many years I lived one way, and now I live this way. Things change."

Grace waited patiently while I struggled to get my question out, because once I said it, if she said no or even hesitated, I would be bitterly disappointed.

But I wasn't. The minute I told her about Jack's idea, Grace started giggling and clapping her hands like she used to do when she was a little girl.

"Oh, Gammy, this is the best idea ever."

"You won't hate living here with me?"

The shocked look on her face astonished me.

"How could you ever think that? I love this house! I love spending time with you! Besides, I could put a little art studio upstairs in what used to be mom's room, if you don't mind that, and it would be so lovely."

"Of course I don't mind," I choked out. "Will your mother be okay with this?"

Grace assured me that her mom would be happy about it, and besides that, it would leave her and Jack in the house together. She'd be happy about that, too.

For the rest of the morning, I was in heaven. Grace called Jack, and he came over, and the three of us discussed how to renovate the house. He would do the downstairs first, so I could move there while they fixed the upstairs, and while they were at it, renovate the kitchen just a bit.

Jack went to his truck, came back with stacks of catalogs of bathroom and kitchen fixtures, and I spent a happy hour planning what I wanted. Not once during that time did I worry about what Peggy was finding out or where Harry went. Or the key, or my mother's death. For an entire hour, I was not worried at all about anything.

When we asked him about a timeline, Jack promised that by the time Grace came home from college on her first visit, the house would be ready. In the meantime, I would have to put up with a little noise. And dirt. And people. But I knew the result would be worth it.

Jack and Grace suggested I get a cleaning service to come in once a week to keep the house relatively clean. I didn't know why I hadn't thought of that before. Cleaning the house had never been my top priority, and that meant there were parts of the house that were always dirtier than the few rooms I tried to clean myself.

I thought about how sometimes the simplest things escape our attention. I knew that thought didn't just apply to the idea of hiring a cleaning service, but to what was going on with Bonnie.

I had planned to ask Jack more about himself, but I never got the chance. Faye called and asked if I wanted to go to lunch, and when I said Grace was with me, she said to bring her along.

It was good that I did. Because within hours, my happy morning would turn into a painful afternoon. Peggy came back from where she'd been and told us all the story of my mother's death and how the world as we knew it tilted a little.

The sharp contrast between the morning's lightness and the afternoon's revelations highlighted the intricate dance between joy and sorrow, past and present.

The story of my mother's death, as unfolded by Peggy, turned out to be more than a recounting of a tragic event. It was a pivotal moment that redefined our understanding of our shared history and individual paths.

I can't say that I was happy about it, but I knew I had asked for the truth, and now that I was learning it, I couldn't return to hiding from it.

Forty Eight

Peggy met us for lunch, but she didn't tell us the news while we were at lunch. Instead, she insisted we eat, drink, and be merry. Probably because she knew I wouldn't feel much like doing either after she told me the news.

Instead, she wanted to talk about Jack's plan for the house and Fayes' work at the allotments. I resisted at first. I could tell that Peggy was wound up inside, just waiting to speak. She looked more tired than I had seen her in a long time, but I finally gave up and went with the flow.

Grace kept looking at the three of us, not aware of where Peggy had gone or why. I wasn't sure that I wanted her to hear what Peggy was going to tell us. But then I decided it was probably best that way. I wouldn't have to repeat anything.

So we had a lovely lunch, and then we walked to the park across the street. I always thought it was wonderful that Whispering Pines had small parks around town. Faye had only recently told me, or reminded me, that I was the one who paid for the extras the parks needed.

I might have paid for it, but it was Harry and Faye who set it up, and Faye made sure the funds were available. So truthfully, I was pretty useless and couldn't claim to have done anything at all.

As we crossed the street, I saw Harry sitting on a bench under the huge oak tree that had been in the park for hundreds of years. He wasn't happy. That's when I knew that what Peggy would tell us would not be good.

As we walked by, I longed to reach out and touch him, but he smiled and vanished, and I looked away to hide my tears. Faye touched my hand, and I wondered how she knew what had happened.

Peggy led us to a picnic table in the small gazebo. Grace sat beside me as we faced Peggy and Faye. I longed to have Bonnie with us too, and I hoped whatever I heard was going to help bring her home.

As Peggy told the story of what she had found, the entire world faded away. My vision and hearing narrowed, so the only thing that existed was the picnic table and Peggy talking.

She explained that since all she had to go by was the fact that my mother died sixty years before, at first it had been difficult to pin down where to get the information. My father hadn't done an obituary. There was no other family but me and him.

It had helped when I told her the date. She had then expanded her search outside of Whispering Pines and finally found the information she was looking for in a town a few hours away called Spring Falls.

It was Grace who said, "Wait, isn't that where Jack grew up?"

Peggy had paused and looked away for a moment before continuing, which scared me. How could Jack be part of this? That was impossible. He was too young. It was just a coincidence.

But when Peggy said that she discovered Bonnie grew up there too, I was sure it wasn't. But what did it mean?

"Did you find Bonnie? Was she there?" Grace asked.

Peggy shook her head, asking to be allowed to tell the story in her way.

Grace settled back on the bench and reached out to hold my hand. I was so grateful for her and worried about what Peggy would say; I couldn't speak.

Peggy said that once she got to Spring Falls, she went directly to someone who could help. And of course, that meant Peggy went to the mayor.

I smiled at that. I imagine a stodgy mayor meeting Peggy for the first time. It would be like an explosion of color and vitality.

But it turned out the mayor was a tall, beautiful woman with red hair that flamed when she was angry, and she and Peggy hit it off immediately.

For a minute, Peggy gushed about the mayor, Judith Zoe, explaining that Judith was too young to know anything about my mother's death but that she had some amazing stories of her own about how she became mayor.

I could tell that Peggy was about to launch into one of those stories, so I said, "But what did you find out about my mother?"

Peggy sagged a little. I was sorry to make her go through the telling, but I was feeling nauseous, giddy, and angry all at the same time. I needed to hear what she had to say and get it over with.

Taking a deep breath, Peggy continued. "Well, Judith finally found the information in the library on microfiche.

"As you know, a drunk driver killed your mother. But it wasn't just one person in the car. A teenager who had been out drinking with his friends hit your mother. There were four of them in the car. All underage.

"It was a town tragedy. Judith found some old-timers who remembered it. They talked about what happened to the four kids. They charged the driver with vehicular homicide. He went to prison. After he got out, no one knew where he went. Because the other three were so young, the court did not send them to prison but placed them on some kind of probation. After it was over, two of them moved away. One stayed in Spring Falls."

When Peggy stopped talking, I waited. But when she just kept looking at the table, I finally asked what seemed to me to be the most important question.

"Why was my mother a few hours away on my birthday?"

Peggy looked relieved. Maybe I had asked the wrong question.

"It's only conjecture, since there was no one there to ask, but at the time there was a pastry shop that made beautiful specialty birthday cakes. And your mother had a slip of paper with that address with her when she died."

It was good that we were sitting outside because I started wailing. Out loud. I didn't mean to. But there it was, coming out of my mouth without my permission.

My mother had been getting me a birthday cake. And she died. It had been all my fault.

I remembered asking for it! I had heard about special cakes and asked if I could have one. Of course, I didn't know that would mean she would choose to buy it instead of make it.

I didn't know that it would be in a town hours away where she would die. Of course, I didn't know that, but it didn't make any difference.

And because now I saw another reason—although my father had loved me—he had kept me at a distance,. It was because of me that my mother, his wife, had died.

All of that broke my heart, and the fear that it was only the beginning of the bad news scared me so much that I shouted my sorrow and fear out loud. Me—the person who tried to hide away and had retreated into my shell for years—was now grieving so loudly that everyone in the park turned to look.

I was so embarrassed, but I couldn't stop until Grace, Peggy, and Faye surrounded me and kept whispering that I was okay.

Finally, after what felt like years, the noise and tears stopped. I took the tissue Grace handed me and said I was ready for the rest of the news. I was lying, of course. Because although I knew there was more to hear, I also knew it wouldn't be good.

Forty Nine

I might have wanted to hear more, but Peggy said no. That was enough for the day. What I didn't know and only found out later was that Peggy wanted to talk to Jack first.

Jack was the pivot point of everything that was going on. That's what I realized that night as I lay in bed, reviewing what Peggy had told me. I talked to myself as I lay there, reminding myself that I was not responsible for my mother's death, my grief and guilt did not go together. It didn't really help, though. To me, they did.

That night, Harry sat at the end of the bed and smiled at me. I wished he would talk. I wished I could ask him questions, and he would tell me everything I needed to know.

Like why hide a box in the lilac bush? What was the key? Why not just tell me things instead of being so secretive? And what did he tell me before he left that last time?

And for heaven's sake, why did he make the bookcase into a magic eye picture? That was the question I whispered to him as I drifted off to sleep.

The next morning, I was back to wondering why I couldn't just fall down the stairs and break my neck. I thought I had moved on, but here I was again. The only trouble was that it would be harder to fall now.

I was stronger. The banister no longer wobbled, and there were treads on the stairs. There was no falling today. Instead, I cursed out loud with each step. There was no one to hear me, anyway.

Except for Harry, who was waiting at the bottom as if he could catch me if I fell. Right, a ghost, an illusion, a spirit—call him whatever name you wish—would not be catching anything. But it helped me to see him. And that's obviously why he was there.

"Can't you just move on? Or talk to me?" I yelled at him.

I was tired of the whole thing. If I hadn't had the list calling to me from the tree table where I had slammed it last night before going to bed, I might have slipped back into my old ways.

But there was Bonnie's name. Still missing. Bring Bonnie home. There was a mystery to be solved, and dang it, I was going to solve it. *Or die trying*, I thought. And then I countered that thought. *There was no dying going on.*

My house would be transformed, Grace would be my roommate, the key would unlock something wonderful, Bonnie would come home again, and Jack would help Jenny at least speak to me again. Maybe we would never be friends, but just seeing her once in a while would be heaven.

Pete showed up an hour into my morning. I had forgotten that we had decided that he would stop by weekly to work in the garden. When I saw him outside, I invited him in for coffee and then held the door open a little longer so his wife could come in. Of course, being what she was, Louise could have just walked in, but she smiled in appreciation that I held the door, anyway.

Pete didn't seem to notice that the door remained open a few seconds longer. I wondered if he knew his wife was always with him. He must have sensed it, because he always seemed to be a happy man. Maybe I could learn something from him.

While we sipped coffee, I showed Pete what Jack intended to do with the house. Louise wandered off somewhere. Pete had some ideas about the house that I thought Jack would agree with.

Eventually, we ended up back in the living room, and Pete sat in Harry's old chair. I was getting used to other people sitting there now. Harry couldn't sit there anymore.

"Are you keeping all those books?" Pete asked. What Pete didn't know was that Louise was standing in front of the bookcases, staring at them, not moving.

When I told Pete I probably would because Harry had arranged them like a Magic Eye picture, Pete stared at me and laughed.

"Your husband and I might have had fun together."

"Why?"

"Well, the obvious is that we both love the woods. The path he made was beautiful; I just had to clean it up a little. And I love Magic Eye pictures. My wife and I used to look at them all the time. We had a game of who could see the picture first."

Pete's wife turned around at that and smiled. Without knowing it, Pete looked directly at her and smiled back. Did he know what he was smiling at? Or was it just a feeling of being happy? Then she turned back and pointed at a section of the bookcase. I had no idea what she was pointing at.

Since that first time, I hadn't been able to see any pictures. Now all I saw was a random bunch of books. I was too afraid to touch any of them, afraid of ruining the picture that I couldn't see, anyway.

"Can you see what the picture is?"

Pete stared at the first bookcase and told me what he saw. It was what I had seen the first time. An abstract picture of birds and trees. Very Harry.

Then Pete looked at the second. That was the one I could never fully make out.

"Oh, this one's different. It's pictures of you and Harry and there's a box down in the corner."

"What kind of box?" I asked, knowing that it was where his wife had pointed. She was no longer at the bookcase but standing behind Harry and looking at me.

"Well, if it wasn't imaginary, I'd say it's a box that has a keyhole that looks like the key you found might fit."

Pete and I were so focused on the bookshelf that neither one of us had heard Jack come in the door, just in time to hear what Pete said about the box.

"What box?" Jack asked.

After explaining the whole Magic Eye thing, Jack didn't look at us as if we were crazy. Instead, he asked, where is the picture of the box?

"Well, I can't see it anymore, but it was over here," Pete said, walking to the bookcase.

"Do you mind?" Jack asked.

I nodded at him to go ahead. I knew what he was thinking.

Jack carefully lifted the books out and put them on the floor in the same order. I knew he was trying to make sure he could put the picture back the same way.

Finally, he found what he was looking for. A real box. With a keyhole.

Jack reached into his pocket, took the key out of the plastic bag, and, looking up at me, inserted the key into the lock.

It fit.

"Stop," I said. "I need a moment."

Fifty

Time stopped. For me anyway,. For Pete and Jack, what happened next lasted only a few minutes. After putting the box on the tree table, they stepped outside, saying they would be there when I was ready.

When I found them later, they were walking through the garden as Pete explained to Jack what he was doing with it for me. There were two men in my life planning ways to improve my life, while the third did his best to ruin it. I knew that wasn't true. But I was still angry with Harry, and that's how I reasoned it out.

Later, they told me what they had worked out. Jack would fix the pergola roof that hung over part of the patio, and Pete would fix the wobbly stones and plant wisteria that would climb the pergola. Harry had said he would do that, but he never got around to it.

But while they were discussing what to do in my backyard, I was somewhere else. I was still in my house, not somewhere else at the same time. I was with Louise and Harry. And they talked to me. Finally. I suppose they could have talked to me before, but I wasn't ready.

But once Jack found that box, I was pretty much ready for anything. Including talking to people who weren't there. Of course, I did it all the time, but now I wanted it to be different. I wanted to hear words. Because all the dead people I talked to before never spoke out loud. It was always silent. I called it mind-talking. It was how I spoke to myself, too, unless I was cursing out loud.

As a dead person, Harry had always been silent. There were no words in my head. I had to guess what he was thinking. Another reason I was often angry at him.

Louise, like most polite dead people, had mind-talked with me before. She was the one who told me her name, when she had confirmed the obvious that she was Pete's wife. But other than that, we had very little reason to communicate.

This time, with Louise and Harry standing in front of me, the bookcase just visible through them, Louise was the first one to speak. She thanked me for giving Pete a place to practice his special gifts and a place where he felt safe and wanted. It had never occurred to me that I was helping Pete, so I thanked her for telling me.

"I'll leave you two to talk," she said as she leaned towards me and gave me what would have been a hug if we were on the same plane of existence. Instead, I only experienced the feeling of it, which was more than enough.

"Oh, and although I just met Harry, I see he is a good man," she said as she drifted out the door towards Pete.

Harry stood waiting, as he had been doing for all these years. To me, he looked the same as he always had. Although I knew we had grown old together, I had never looked at him as anything other than the same man I had loved since he was a boy.

We didn't speak for a moment. I was afraid of saying the wrong thing, and I knew he felt the same way. Although I felt angry at him for leaving and for not telling me things, I loved him with all of my being.

Finally, I just asked, "Why?"

I meant all the whys. Why did he travel so much? Why did he go off into the woods to die? Why was he still around but not talking? Why did he hide something in the box and not just tell me that day when we planted the lilac bush together?

Outside, a flurry of white petals flew by the window. Well, not flew, really. Since time had slowed down for me, they moved in slow motion. A bird floated by, glancing in the window at me as he headed to the feeder hanging on a branch of the maple tree. I wondered if he could see Harry.

Still, Harry didn't speak. He just stood and looked at me the same way he had always looked at me. With love in his eyes.

What was he waiting for?

Gesturing to our chairs, Harry moved to his, and I moved to mine. It was like old times; our chairs swiveled to look out the window while keeping each other in view. Except Harry didn't make a dent in his chair.

Finally, Harry spoke. His voice sounded exactly the same. Deep and round. When we'd speak on the phone, I could feel the vibrations inside me as if I were a tuning fork.

This felt the same way, but even better. I didn't hear his words outside of me; I heard them as part of me.

"I should have told you instead of hiding it in a box," Harry said. "But I did tell you, right before I died. It's what you forgot. When you open the box, you'll remember it again. But this time, you are stronger."

I waved my hand in protest.

"You are. And you have your friends. And Grace. And Jenny in her own way."

"What could be so bad that I chose to forget, and you chose to hide it from me all these years?" I asked my dead husband.

"I didn't mean to hide it all those years. I arranged the books so you would see the picture. I thought of it more as a scavenger hunt. I thought you'd find it while I was still here to talk about it.

"But you didn't. So I told you what was in it. I'm sorry, Mabel."

That was the last thing I heard before he vanished. Time went back to normal. A car door slammed. Moments later, Faye and Peggy opened the front door without knocking.

I was still in my chair. I swiveled to face them and said, "Are you here about the box?"

"Jack called," Faye said. She was calm. Peggy was not. I could see her car parked in the driveway.

"How fast did you drive?" I laughed.

The three of us burst out laughing. I wasn't even going to bother to explain what had happened. What was important was that they were there. I was moving on, and the box was waiting to be opened.

Whatever I had been afraid of wasn't enough to stop me from living my best life right now. At least, that's what I told myself as we joined the men outside. Faye handed the box to Jack, and he turned the key.

Fifty One

If I thought that some magic fairy dust would fly out of the box when it was opened, I was sorely disappointed. The lid creaked and then flopped back onto the table.

Inside, there were two black plastic boxes. One of them rattled when I picked it up. Looking inside, I laughed. I had wondered where Jenny's baby teeth had gone. Harry had always loved playing the tooth fairy. If one of Jenny's teeth fell out when he was gone, I'd have to explain that the tooth fairy was busy, and she'd have to wait since he was on the other side of the world.

We both pretended that she didn't already know that it was her dad. We'd giggle and snuggle together and read the books that Harry would buy her before he would leave. A tear dropped onto my hand. Jenny and I had such lovely times together when she was a little girl.

Inside the other box was a folded-up piece of paper. It was a newspaper clipping.

Peggy knew what it was even before I started to unfold it.

"Sit down," she said, taking it out of my hand.

I did. We all did. And then Peggy read the article. She had seen it before on the microfiche in Spring Falls, so she knew what it said. It described the accident that killed my mother.

And it listed the names of the children—because that's what they were—who had killed her. Sixteen-year-olds who were stupid and drunk. Before she read the last name, Peggy hesitated and then said, "I'm sorry, Jack," before saying his mother's name.

None of us knew why she said she was sorry. Jack had never shared his mother's name with us. So when he turned white and stood, his chair falling to the ground behind him, we stared at him as if he had gone crazy.

Peggy whispered to Pete, Faye, and me, "His mother."

It was my turn to stand. I grabbed Jack's wrist so he wouldn't run. He flinched. But how could I be mad at him? I never understood how people blamed someone for what one of their loved ones did. He hadn't even been born yet.

I pulled him close into a hug, and we stood there for a moment. He was so tall he had to bend over to hug me, and I did my best to comfort him.

"Sit," Faye said to the two of us, and she went to turn the kettle on. Faye knew my kitchen as well as I did, probably better, since she was the one who had organized it for me one day. She said the lack of order was making her crazy, and I willingly relinquished my ownership of how it was so she could make it better.

In some ways, I was good at letting go. In other ways, not so much. Probably why Harry had been afraid of telling me how my mother died. But now, having learned of it the day before from Peggy, I wasn't as shattered. Although Jack's mother being one of the children in the car, that was shocking, to say the least. What were the odds?

But there was no way to go back and change the past. None of us knew that me wanting a special birthday cake would get my mother killed. And it certainly wasn't Jack's fault. As Jack and I sat back down at the table for the first time since she died, I saw my mother.

Had she been waiting all this time for me to know what happened and then let go of the guilt? She raised her hand, blew me a kiss, the same way she used to when I was a child when I was heading off to school, and then vanished.

Perhaps she was free to go because I was finally giving up resentments and growing up. I felt as if I could handle anything.

It was Jack who needed the tea. But we all drank it together. Even Pete, who really didn't understand all that was happening, went along with it anyway. I saw Faye smile at him and then look directly at Louise and smile.

Could Faye see Louise, or was it just a sense that someone was there? Either way, I planned on quizzing her later. But what happened next astonished me. Louise leaned over, kissed Pete on the cheek, turned to Faye, blew her a kiss, and vanished.

Louise was gone? Had she turned her husband over to Faye? I could see why, if that's what she had done. Faye would be the perfect companion for him, and now that my eyes were opened, I could see how much she liked him.

Jack turned to me, and he said, "My mother never told me what the accident was or who died. I'm so sorry, Mabel."

"Nothing to be sorry about, Jack. And I think it's good that we know now. I can see how the universe, in all its wisdom, has brought you into our lives. It kind of makes you a part of the family, doesn't it?"

I didn't mean Jack and Jenny, but as I said it, I realized it was true. Jack was part of our family. Grace already treated him like he was her dad, and he felt like the son I had never had. I didn't need Jenny to marry him for it to feel that way.

A tap on the window brought me back to the present.

"Anyone want to go for a walk with me and my ravens?"

To my surprise and delight, everyone did. So instead of just me trundling down the street to the lake following a raven, there were five of us. We waved at the neighbors, and they waved back.

I wasn't sure if I had ever been that happy before.

But not completely, because Bonnie was still missing. And I was sure her disappearance had something to do with Jack. And, I was sure, Spring Falls. But what?

Grace had texted as we walked to the lake, so she was waiting for us when we got there. If it surprised her to see Pete, Jack, Faye, and Peggy with me, she didn't show it.

Instead, she waited, and as we walked, she dropped back to talk to me, reaching out to hold my hand, just like she and her mother had done when they were little girls.

Until that moment, I hadn't realized how much I missed that feeling of a hand in mine. What a gift to give someone. Just holding hands. So simple.

The sunlight filtered through the June green leaves on the tree, making patterns on the ground and highlighting the forest floor. Tiny flowers poked their heads out through the leaf litter left over from the fall, and a squirrel scampered in the leaves beside us before running up a tree. Jay and Dove were far ahead of us, scouting the way.

It was Grace who said what I was thinking: "Now we still have to find Bonnie."

"We will," I answered. But I was worried. What could be so bad that Bonnie felt she had to run away instead of telling us?

Fifty Two

The next few days were full of activity. Whatever plans were going on for my upcoming birthday, they were not being shared with me. The only thing I knew was the time and the place. Everything else was happening without me.

Like life, I thought, once I realized I was not in charge of what was going to happen. Why had I ever thought that I was anyway? Looking back, I could see how nothing I had planned had worked out the way I thought it would.

But if I looked at my life without resentment, guilt, or disappointment, I could see that it had all been perfect. It was how I reacted to each thing that happened that made a difference. Free will, I thought. Maybe that was what it meant. I could choose.

When Grace asked me what I wanted for my birthday, I said there was nothing I needed. Having everyone together in harmony would be more than enough. So indirectly, I told her what I wanted, and I knew she understood.

I wanted Bonnie to come home. I wanted Jenny to at least speak to me. She didn't have to like me or love me as her mother. I just wanted to have her back in my life. Maybe like a casual friend. That would be enough.

If there was any progress in finding Bonnie, no one shared that with me. And Jack had already promised to talk to Jenny. If he couldn't help heal the rift between us, I wasn't sure anyone could.

Jack had become a permanent fixture in my day. He arrived the first thing in the morning, along with his crew, who had already started turning the dining room into a bedroom and making the downstairs bathroom bigger.

As he had warned me it would be, the house was loud and dirty. However, he promised me the worst of it would be over in a few days, as he had everyone working on it because he wanted the bedroom and bathroom done before my birthday.

That seemed impossible to me, but when I saw how many people showed up on the first day and the mess that they made, I could see how they might pull it off—at least enough so that it wouldn't feel like living inside an airplane engine.

But Peggy and Faye had worked out a solution. They took turns picking me up when the crew arrived, and I spent the day with them. It started with Faye. We went to her house, where she made me the best coffee and muffins I had ever had.

For the next hour, she went over my accounts with me. She promised we would do that at least once a week. It was time for me to take back a little more control over where my money went and why.

Then we headed off to the allotments, where she and I provided support to anyone that needed it. Faye answered questions about different plants, how to grow them, and how to protect them against invasive insects without pesticides.

I didn't know that the allotments didn't allow any kind of spraying. That made sense. There was no way to protect one allotment from another. What one person did affected another.

"Like life," Faye said later when I asked her about it. "Everything one person does affects another. It isn't so clearly defined as people growing vegetables side by side, but it still works that way."

"But how do you know what the right thing is to do all the time?" I had asked her later, as we finished up the day at her house, eating an early dinner.

"Well, we don't, but we can choose to do our best to do the next right thing. And I often remember something that the writer Ursula K. Le Quinn had posted over her desk."

Leading me back to her tiny office beside her bedroom, I saw she had posted the same thing over her desk.

"Is it true? Is it necessary or at least useful? Is it compassionate or at least unharmful?"

I asked her to write it out for me, and I put it in my purse beside my list. But first, I showed the list to Faye. It amazed me how much I had gotten done, or at least was diligently working on. I mentally gave myself a pat on the back.

When Faye brought me home, Jack was the only person there. The crew was gone. A huge dumpster sat in the yard, filled with what I assumed had been the walls of my bedroom and bathroom. I could see the corner of the rug sticking out of the top.

"Don't worry, that will be picked up tomorrow," Jack said as he held the door for me.

Everything in the living room was neat and tidy. Seeing my face, Jack said the crew had cleaned before they left. Taking my hand, he led me to what was going to be my bedroom. There were new walls and windows in both the bedroom and bathroom.

I couldn't believe it. It was already a brand new space. As I stared in wonder, Jack explained that the wooden floors, now revealed once the rug was gone, would be sanded and stained in the morning, and then the walls would be painted.

The new appliances would be installed in the bathroom, which was now much bigger because they had knocked the wall out between the bathroom and a closet. The closet was now one entire wall of my bedroom.

I could see that I was going to love my new downstairs bedroom and bathroom.

"How did you do all this?" I asked, my mouth hanging open in astonishment.

"A good crew who worked together," was his answer.

Two valuable life lessons in one day, I thought to myself, wondering what the next day would bring.

It was both what I expected and what I didn't. Like life.

Fifty Three

My day with Peggy was completely different from my day with Faye. With Peggy, everything was exhausting and exhilarating at the same time. Instead of a quiet coffee and muffins in Faye's fairy cottage, we went to a local diner where everyone knew Peggy. And apparently, many of them knew me too.

Even though I had begun to remember people, every secret revealed seemed to open a door to my memory. There were some people who still seemed like strangers to me. But I wasn't a stranger to them. They'd come over and say how much they missed seeing me up and about, or smile and wave from across the room.

I had become quite good at pretending to know people, even if I didn't remember them. And if a dead person was hanging around with them, that would sometimes jog my memory. The unspoken question was always, did I see someone with them? But I wasn't comfortable blurting that out.

When Peggy casually asked me how many dead people were in the room with us, I choked on my coffee, and she had to rub my back until I stopped wheezing.

Then, with wide eyes and her face framed by a butterfly scarf that was holding back her hair, she giggled and said, "Of course we know there are other people here, you silly woman. You used to be more forthcoming about it than you are now."

"I used to talk about it?" I stuttered, looking at all the people around me.

"Well, not all the time to everyone. But mostly everyone. You have comforted many of the people in this room. So how could they not know what you see?"

Indeed, I thought. *How could they not know*? What still made little sense to me was how I could forget all this. Was it the trauma of learning how my mother died, thinking it was because of me, and then Harry leaving?

Was I that self-centered that those two events stopped me from using this strange gift I had to help people? Eleven years was a long time to be vacant from my life, especially since I was obviously in the last quarter of it. Or perhaps I had no time left, since no one knew when they would leave this plane of existence.

Not knowing when it would be was a given. Most people didn't have a warning. I was always meeting people who had passed on and didn't know that they had because it had been sudden. Or they knew, but refused to accept that they had died.

Dead wasn't really an appropriate term for what happened. It only looked like death to people living on this plane of existence. The body ceased to function. The person didn't. But since they were no longer interacting with us and very few people could see them, it looked like death.

But life couldn't die. I didn't understand the spiritual or physics reason for this fact. I just knew it to be true. So when Harry "died," I tried to follow him by just giving up. Obviously, that hadn't worked.

And I was really too much of a coward to let myself fall down the stairs. I knew a fall wasn't a guarantee. I might not die. I could just be injured, and living in pain was the last thing that I wanted. Instead, I gave up everything that made me useful and valuable to the world. I suppose that is also a form of death.

Now I was trying to follow Peggy and Faye back into life. And it was working. I thoroughly enjoyed my day with Peggy, even though it was exhausting. We visited a few homes she had for sale, a bookstore, and a boutique grocery store that sold her favorite kind of pasta.

We had an early dinner at the restaurant where Grace worked, so I had a chance to see her. She had been busy working on the birthday party. As I watched Grace interact with the guests she was serving, I marveled once again at how skilled she was at putting people at ease.

She certainly didn't get that gift from me, I thought, but then I reminded myself that perhaps that wasn't true. Perhaps it was just what I had been telling myself, so I didn't feel guilty for giving up.

By the time Peggy brought me home, I was ready for bed. Once again, the crew had left, and only Jack remained in the house. Although the bathroom wasn't entirely put together, the bedroom was, and the crew had brought my bed downstairs for me.

When Jack opened the door to show me my room, I gasped. I could feel tingles running up and down my body. For the first time, I understood what people meant when they said they tingled all over.

In all my life, I had never had a room that felt like it belonged just to me. Everything was perfect. I knew it was Faye who had done it, and since Peggy was behind me giggling a little, I knew she had a hand in it, too.

The walls were the faintest shade of lilac. White, filmy curtains fluttered with the breeze coming through the open windows. The bed had a new bedspread which was the same color as the walls. A vase of flowers sat on the dresser. And when Jack slid open the closet doors, I saw that all my clothes were inside.

It was so beautiful. I burst into tears.

And then I felt Faye's arm around me and realized she must have been in the kitchen, waiting to surprise me.

"So, you kind of like it?" Faye asked.

Then I started laughing, and Jack, Faye, and Peggy joined in.

Although it was still only early evening, I said, "Could I go to bed now?"

Even though that made everyone laugh harder, I was absolutely serious. My favorite books were on the end table, and a new reading light was installed above my bed. Everything was ready for me.

"Not yet," Jack said, showing me the bathroom. Although the toilet and sink worked, the tile was not done, and the shower wasn't finished, but it was perfect. I didn't have to go upstairs to get anything. Now it would be really hard to fall down the stairs and break my neck.

Instead, I'd have Grace's company when she was home.

"This is the best present I've ever had," I told the three of them. And I meant it.

Jack assured me all the downstairs work would be done by the end of the next day, and it wouldn't take them long to spruce up the upstairs for Grace. He reminded me that Pete would come over in the morning to work on the garden. By my birthday, everything would be done.

If I hadn't seen how fast they had done the downstairs, I wouldn't have believed it. After all, my birthday was only two days away. But it appeared that Jack had some kind of magical wand, so I simply nodded and gave him the biggest hug I could.

I heard Faye and Peggy gasp a little. I was not a hugger. I even surprised myself with that hug. But how could I not? Life was almost perfect.

All I needed was for Bonnie to come back, and whatever was going on between Bonnie and Jack to be cleared up. Given all that had happened so far, that didn't seem like such a big thing to ask.

And Jenny to talk to me, I added. Just in case someone was listening.

227

Fifty Four

The next morning, I thought perhaps I had died after all. I didn't know where I was. I looked for Harry. If I were dead, he should be there. But he wasn't. Perhaps I wasn't. I couldn't imagine Harry wouldn't be right beside me the moment I moved to his realm.

It took a few minutes to remember that I was in my new bedroom. The bed was facing a different direction, the faint light coming in through the window was slanted against a different wall, and the smell of flowers filled the room.

It was the vase of flowers that Faye had put on the dresser that brought me fully awake. She had chosen flowers where the scents of each harmonized with each other. I hadn't realized before that a vase of flowers was like a song.

No silly, I said to myself, *everything is a song.* It was nature that made the most beautiful song. Humans did a piss-poor job of it most times. Sitting up, I thought about how unhappy ugly places made me and realized it was because they were out of harmony.

No wonder most people are grumpy, frustrated, and angry, I thought, and I wondered if I could do anything about it. *Not really,* I realized. The only thing I could do was try to be more harmonious myself. That made me question if that meant I had to stop cursing.

I decided that less would probably be better. Otherwise, it would be like cymbals crashing together all the time rather than punctuating the music in the right place.

Humph, I grumbled, and then laughed. What a stupid thing to grumble about. *Harmony,* I reminded myself. I put on the clothes I had laid out the night before, visited the bathroom, stared at the old woman in the mirror and not for the first time wondered how that had happened.

It was easy to get to the kitchen. All I had to do was walk out the bedroom door and turn left. I could see the garden through the glass door that led outside and realized that a deep fog had rolled in. Although I kind of missed the trip down the stairs, I knew I wouldn't miss it for long.

While I waited for the coffee, I wondered what was bothering me. Was someone in the house? I looked around. There were no dead people there. I didn't expect there to be someone. Long ago, I had put up a barrier around the house that didn't allow that to happen. Of course Harry had been allowed in, and obviously Louise, but she had come in through Pete, so she wasn't a stranger.

I loved my privacy and didn't like the thought that I would wake up and someone would be waiting for me. But that's exactly how it felt then. I told myself I was just discombobulated because of the changes in the house.

With a coffee cup in one hand and a muffin in the other, I glanced at the clock that also displayed the outside temperature. Judging that it was warm enough to go outside, despite the fog, I stepped outside just as the fog started to lift.

Putting the coffee and muffin down on the table, I used the dish towel I had so thoughtfully thought to bring outside with me to wipe down the table and chair. As I turned to sit, once again I felt the presence of someone else.

It was good I had put the coffee and muffin down because otherwise I would have dropped them both. I think I screamed a little when I saw who was sitting on the bench under the maple tree.

Bonnie stood and gave me a tentative smile. Forgetting that I hated running, I ran towards her, for a moment afraid that she was just another ghost. But as my arms went around her and I smelled her scent, I started to cry. She was real. And in my backyard. Then she started to cry, and we were two old women crying in the garden.

After the first shock and the feeling of gratitude for her return, I got angry. I yelled at her for scaring me and then for staying away.

Bonnie had let me rant for a minute, and then she said she was sorry. The tears had started again, and as she told me her story, they continued. Then, as she spoke, I remembered what Harry had told me before he died.

It was about Bonnie. But I didn't tell her I remembered. I didn't tell her then what Harry had found out. I didn't tell her what I had known, but had run away from the knowing. The anger returned, but this time it was at myself.

Just then, Jay and Dove flew overhead, their wings casting a shadow on the ground. The illusion was perfect. I saw four birds instead of two. Two in the air, and two below me as shadows. That broke the spell. All the anger, frustration, and sorrow I felt were just shadows. A waste of time. What was real contained none of that.

By the time Pete arrived, I had remembered everything, and I had forgiven both myself, Harry, and even Bonnie for keeping secrets.

I introduced the two of them and then told Pete to tell Jack that Bonnie was back and I was going over to Faye's. We didn't tell him we were leaving because we didn't want to be there when Jack arrived, but I could tell Pete knew. What he didn't know was why.

Bonnie and I were fully aware that sooner or later Bonnie would have to share her story with Jack, but she wasn't ready yet.

I wasn't ready either. There was no way to know how Jack would react, and I realized I loved having him around, and what Bonnie had to say might end our relationship.

I texted Faye that I was coming over and asked her to get Peggy to come over, too. At the last minute, I added, "I have Bonnie with me."

A row of exclamation marks and hearts was her response.

It was exactly how I felt.

Fifty Five

Peggy arrived at Faye's at the same time we drove up. She had barely stopped before she was out of her car and running towards us. Because she was wearing the brightest pink outfit I had ever seen with a green scarf tied around her hair, she looked like a running tulip.

The moment Bonnie stopped the car, Peggy pulled her out and hugged her so hard that I heard Bonnie squeak. Then Peggy did what I had done. Got mad. She stepped back, hands on her hips and said, "How could you scare us like that!"

Bonnie stood her ground. Her white hair shimmering in the sunlight, waiting for the storm to pass, which it did within moments. Peggy hugged her again, and the three of us walked toward Faye.

Faye had waited in her doorway, calmly watching over us like the protector that she is. Walking towards her was like moving towards a song. You could almost feel the vibrations of it, as if it surrounded her entire house. Which, knowing Faye, it probably did.

If Peggy looked like a tulip, Faye was the violet singing of the beauty of the world. I wondered if anyone had ever been mad at Faye. Or Faye mad at them.

Although I had been at Faye's just a few days before, it appeared everything in her back garden had bloomed as if a few weeks had gone by. I could see why Louise felt comfortable leaving her husband, Pete, in Faye's hands. They would build many beautiful gardens together.

Once we were settled with our tea and the tiny scones that were Faye's specialty, Peggy asked to hear the entire story.

Faye stopped us by holding up her hand. "I know you have heard it already, Mabel, and we want to hear it, but I think we are missing the one person who needs to hear it."

"You knew?" Bonnie asked, staring at Faye.

"Pretty obvious, don't you think?" Faye said, holding Bonnie's hand.

"Well, not to me," Peggy said as she gave us all that look I remember so well from our high school days.

"I didn't think it was obvious," I said. There was no way I was going to tell Peggy right then that I had known, but forgot. On purpose, coward that I am.

What I didn't know yet was how Harry had known. That part I either never knew or it could be added to the list of what I had refused to remember. Maybe Bonnie knew.

I looked over at Bonnie, and she said, "You're right. Call Jack. And I'll tell the complete story. Including the part I left out about Harry."

Fifty Six

"Hey," Jack said as he answered his phone. "Pete said you went to Faye's, and Bonnie came back. Great news!"

In the background, I could hear Jack moving around my house, and I imagined him directing the workers as they came in the door.

"Yes. It is. Say, Jack, could you come over to Faye's right now?"

Jack must have heard something in my voice because he didn't hesitate and just added that Grace had just come in the door, and should she come too?

Grace. I hadn't thought about Grace. She needed to know because she would be part of the aftermath, and of course she loved Bonnie too.

I barely squeezed out the word "yes" before hanging up. I probably scared Jack by doing that because the two of them were at Faye's within minutes, looking worried.

Peggy had waited for them out front, and I heard the anxiety in Grace's voice, asking what was going on. And Peggy—bless her ability to smooth over any situation—said something that made Grace smile as she came into Faye's garden.

Jack looked uncomfortable. I wondered if it was just because he was the only man in a group of women who must have looked very serious, or if he had an inkling of what was going to happen.

We made small talk while Faye brought out coffee for Jack, tea for Grace, and another plate of scones. Grace picked one up and declared it one of her favorite things to eat, making all our hearts a little lighter as we watched her enjoy the treat.

Bonnie cleared her throat, and we all looked her way. Bonnie was always pale, but she had turned so pale now that I worried for her. But it had to be done, and she knew it.

She started off by apologizing to Jack for the story she was going to tell. I didn't think she needed to apologize; she had done nothing wrong. But I knew what she meant. She was about to share something that could change his life. It would be for the better. But would he see it that way?

Bonnie reminded Jack that she grew up in Spring Falls, just like he did. Her parents had died not long after she had moved to Whispering Pines. But even before then, they had not had a close relationship.

"It got worse when I was sixteen," Bonnie said. "Back in those days, if a girl claimed she was raped, either no one believed her or told her it was her fault. It's a little better now, but then it was a given that she wouldn't get much support."

"Oh no," Grace said. "Is that what happened to you?"

"It did."

This was Bonnie, the teacher. Telling a story as if it happened to someone else. It was probably the only way she could get through it. I sent her a smile of support, but she was so focused she didn't see it.

Although I had already heard the story, I could feel tears well up, and I saw how everyone else looked. Grace had tears running down her face. I knew her best friend had been raped in high school, and she had stayed by her friend's side through the ordeal of trying to tell her side of the story. It hadn't gone well.

Jack reached out and took Grace's hand. She smiled at him, and I prayed he would take the rest of the story as a gift. Grace and my daughter needed him in their lives.

Turning to Peggy, Bonnie added, "After you went to Spring Falls, Judith started looking at the accident that killed Mabel's mother. She talked to many people and finally found someone who told her the rest of the story. It's how she found me. She knew where to look. And then she told me to stop running."

"Where did she find you?" Peggy asked.

"My parents kept a small cabin outside of town. I never sold it. Sometimes I rent it out, but it was empty, so I went there."

Taking a deep breath, she continued. "I got pregnant, which only compounded the trouble with my parents. I was sent away until the baby was born and then forced to give him up for adoption."

Turning to Jack, she said, "That's when I met your mother, Jack."

I held my breath as Bonnie continued. Jack had stopped holding Grace's hand, and he was frowning. Not a good sign. He had to see what was coming.

"She and your father were looking to adopt. As you know, she couldn't have children, and you know she blamed herself for killing Mabel's mother. Even though she had only been a passenger in the car,"

By then, everyone knew what Bonnie was going to say next. Jack had become so still he looked like a statue.

"I'm sorry, Jack. But your mom thought that by adopting a child, she could somehow make up for what had happened. Of course, it wasn't her fault. But she couldn't forgive herself for being so young and stupid, even though she was only sixteen when it happened.

"And there she was, looking at another sixteen-year-old, but this one was in trouble through no fault of her own. Unless you call being in the wrong place at the wrong time her fault, which some people did.

"I was like your mother. Our lives had changed at sixteen. Your mother was the kindest woman I had ever met. Your mother, Jack, was my savior."

Jack stood. It was impossible to tell what he was thinking. Then he turned and walked away.

Grace looked at me. Bonnie had crumbled. I knew Grace didn't know if she should stay and help or go after Jack.

"Go," I said.

We could take care of Bonnie. It was Jack who needed someone, and I couldn't think of anyone better than my granddaughter. Grace was the light of my life, and I knew she could be that for Jack too.

Besides, I needed to hear the rest of the story. Because there was one more part to tell. How Harry had known and then told me.

Fifty Seven

"He'll be okay," Faye said. She had her arm around Bonnie, who was sobbing into her shoulder. "It's just the shock of it. He's a good man, and he'll realize what a gift it is to have you in his life. And all of us who come along with the package."

Peggy and I nodded. It was true. Jack had a new life waiting for him, and unless we were all mistaken about who he was, he would eventually realize that. How long that would take was the question. Bonnie's heart had been broken all these years, and it was time for it to be put back together again.

If I had realized anything these past couple of months, it was that keeping secrets and running away from truths would solve nothing. I was going to do my best to stop running from things I didn't want to hear, and listen.

What I needed was more faith in the world's goodness. And there was no reason for me not to have it. I had everything that anyone could want.

And even though Harry's physical presence was gone, who he was remained part of everything in my life. And I knew for a fact that what we called death was just walking into another phase of life.

While I waited for Bonnie to recover, I pulled out my list and crossed off, "Find Bonnie." All I needed now was to have all the answers. What and how had Harry known?

It was as if I had spoken the question out loud.

Bonnie hiccuped, wiped her eyes, and then blew her nose before saying, "Harry knew, and he told me he had told you. But then he died, and you said nothing, so I thought you were embarrassed for me. Or maybe even blamed me for what happened.

"Then, when Jack showed up in town and you still didn't say anything, I assumed you didn't approve and were ashamed of me. So I left. I thought I would make a new life somewhere else. I thought that by returning to where it all happened, I could finally resolve it for myself.

"I had even thought of confronting the man who had raped me. I never had. And no one had ever come forward to help me get closure."

Although I was eager to find out how Harry knew and exactly what he knew, the more important question was the one that Peggy asked.

"Did you find him? Did you get a chance to confront him?"

Bonnie sighed. "It's probably better that I didn't. But I couldn't, anyway. Marshall Ferguson is dead. It's a long story, but it's how Judith became the mayor of Spring Falls. Marshall had been the mayor of Spring Falls for over forty years. That's how much he fooled everyone."

When Bonnie stopped talking, we all paused and looked out into the fairyland of Faye's garden and the amazing beauty of all that was going on. The trees rustling in the warm June wind, two bluebirds sitting on the bluebird house surveying their kingdom, a fat honey bee buried into a nasturtium that grew in a pot beside the table.

It would take forever to list all the tiny, beautiful things that were going on just in that one space, all of them working in harmony. The universe comprised infinitely beautiful ideas, and then there were the discordant ones that caused so much pain.

I didn't understand why they were there, but I knew they didn't deserve the power and attention we gave them.

It was time for the last bit of the puzzle.

"Okay. Harry told me he knew. But what did he know, and how did he find out? Was it so horrific that I chose to forget? For eleven years? My not acknowledging what you believed I knew must have been horrible for you."

"It was, Mabel. At first. But then I saw you freeze up and go inside, and I knew you were suffering much more than me.

"And Harry knew because I told him. I wanted help to find my son. Although I knew Jack's parents, I never knew their real names or where they lived. I wanted it that way. I was afraid that I would regret giving him up and want him back.

"I did regret it. I did want him back. At first. And then, as time went on, I accepted that he was much better off without me, and I knew the couple that adopted him would give him a good life.

"Harry found Jack's adopted parents for me. But he also found out something else. And it was something else that you wanted to forget."

By then, I was getting impatient. I couldn't imagine I would have withdrawn the way I did just because Harry told me about Bonnie.

"What?" I asked, a little too snippy.

"He found out who Grace's father was."

Not knowing Grace's father had always been a point of contention between Jenny and me. I had long ago given up asking. But it sat between us, like a wall.

Even though Jenny had often been unhappy with me, it was only after she came home and had Grace that she had frozen me out.

Choosing to do only what had to be done to be a polite but very distant daughter.

Bonnie stopped talking. But tears started rolling down my checks unchecked, as I let myself remember everything.

I barely spoke the words out loud. "Grace is Jack's sister."

Peggy gasped, Faye dropped her head, and Bonnie nodded.

"Marshall?"

"Marshall," she answered. "He spoke at her college. She thought he was wonderful and went out for a drink afterward with him."

At first, all I could think was that it was good that Marshall was dead. Otherwise, I'd have to find a way to kill him myself. And the second thought was for Grace and Jack.

"They don't know?"

Bonnie shook her head. How could they?

Now all I could think about was how would their relationship survive it? Jenny was in love with the son of a man who raped her, and he was Grace's half-brother.

There was nothing to prevent them from continuing as they were—even getting married, which I knew they wanted to do. Grace had told me. But once they found out the truth, what would happen?

I looked up, horrified that I had run away from helping Jenny. And now that Jack was in the picture, it could become even more of a disaster.

Faye smiled and said, "I'll take care of it." And I had to trust that she could.

All I wanted for the three of them was a happy life together. It didn't seem like too much to ask. Except it just might be.

Fifty Eight

The rest of the day was a blur. I was anxious one minute and crying my eyes out the next. Since Harry's death, I had not felt so much pain. Even Harry's death had not been this painful because I had shut down so I wouldn't have to deal with it.

This time, I didn't run away from it. I let myself grieve for everyone. I let myself feel pain for everyone. For my daughter, my granddaughter, Jack, and my friend Bonnie, who had lived with this secret for years.

I cursed silently and out loud. I yelled at Harry for leaving me. I yelled at myself for letting Jenny down.

And when that was over, I sat in my chair in the living room and waited. There was nothing for me to do. I had to trust that Faye could somehow make everything better. Because this time I wasn't running away.

When night came, I went to bed and tried to sleep, but nothing happened. My body felt as if it was vibrating like a tuning fork. I remembered the feeling. It had happened before, right after Harry's death. All the tricks I knew about sleeping deserted me, just as they had then. So I lay in bed and stared at the tree shadows the moon made on my ceiling.

I must have finally dozed off because the sun was coming in my window when I woke up.

The first thing I did was call Faye and tried to cancel the birthday party. She said absolutely not. So preparations went on. Without me. I wished I had something to do to take my mind off of everything. I tried reading, but the words blurred.

In the afternoon, Faye called. I hadn't seen Jack. The workmen had not arrived that day. So either they were taking the day off, or Jack was refusing to have anything to do with any of us. It was not a good sign.

But Faye had done what I couldn't do. Had the conversation with Jenny, Jack, and Grace. And although I asked how it went, she wouldn't tell me. She said all that was important was that the truth was out in the open, and now everyone could decide how to deal with it.

Although I felt incredibly guilty for not being the one to tell them, I knew it was better this way. Jenny would never have been able to hear what I had to say without all her perceptions and ideas of me getting in the way. And most of them were correct anyway, or had been.

I waited by the phone the rest of the day, praying that at least Grace would call and relieve me of my misery. But she didn't. And I knew I had to wait. I couldn't force the issue, but I wanted so much to be the one that Grace and Jenny turned to to talk about it, that I felt like driving to the house and confronting them.

Jay was the one who stopped me from doing that. And Pete. Faye had told him the entire story, and he came by saying that he was checking on the garden, but I knew he was checking up on me.

When Jay tapped on the kitchen window while we were drinking tea at the table, Pete couldn't believe it. When I told him that Jay wanted me to come out for a walk, Pete stood and pulled me up, saying, "Well, let's go then. I've never had a chance to walk with a raven."

Although I smiled and waved at the neighbors, my heart wasn't in it. But when we reached the lake, everything changed. It felt just like a cheesy metaphor. The clouds parted, and light poured into my life. Because I saw Grace sitting on the bench by the lake waiting for me. Pete hugged me goodbye, bowed to Jay, thanking him for the walk, and I settled myself beside Grace.

"I figured Jay would come get you, and you would know enough to follow him here."

Grace paused, and I waited.

"Granddad knew and told you about mom and you forgot?"

"I'm sorry. I did. When Harry died, I forgot everything. Looking back at it, I remember it feeling like there was a fog in my head. You were a lighthouse that kept bringing me back to life, otherwise, I'm sure I would have found some way to follow Harry."

"Thank you for staying, Gammy. And for making a place in your home for me."

"Forever," I said, pulling Grace close to me.

"I have a brother," Grace said in a whisper.

I waited. Hoping. But she didn't say more about her mother and Jack and I didn't ask. Just having her with me was enough.

Fifty Nine

The next day, I woke up so early that the sun wasn't up yet. There were so many emotions running through me that I couldn't sleep.

After Grace left, I walked home, not knowing anything other than that she would see me at the party. She didn't mention Jenny or Jack.

So I was excited, worried, scared, and hopeful all at the same time. I hadn't seen Bonnie, Faye, or Peggy for two days, and I felt abandoned even though I knew they were preparing the party for me.

And although the workman returned to the house later in the morning, Jack wasn't with them. I tried not to read anything into it, but of course my brain was making up all kinds of stories.

Harry hadn't shown up for days either, and that made me a little mad and very sad, but at the same time, I was happy for him. He had hung around long enough to make sure I returned to the land of the living and remembered everything.

Peggy picked me up to go to the party. I was definitely not in a party mood, but I had learned long ago that no one said no to

Peggy. Besides, my friends had put so much work into it that I couldn't disappoint them.

I had selected a dress that Grace had picked out for me, a flowing floral print, and since it was cold, I added a denim jacket she had convinced me to buy. The woman in the mirror didn't look like me at all, but she wasn't bad-looking, I decided. Especially when she smiled. I remembered Jenny practicing faces in the mirror when she was little, so I tried out a few myself.

Surprisingly, it made me feel better.

Peggy didn't bother coming to the door; she just honked. Which made me laugh and feel like I was in high school again. Peggy waved out the window at me, her arm glittering with all the bracelets she had stacked, and yelled, "Hurry up, slowpoke!"

I realized it was going to be impossible to be gloomy, or discouraged, with Peggy around, so I decided not to be. Whatever happened, it would be okay.

But it was more than okay. It was glorious. Faye's house was full of sparkling lights, and a woman was playing the harp out in the garden.

It looked as if the whole town had come to Faye's home. It took me a minute to realize it looked so crowded because quite a few people had someone else beside them. People I had known before they died.

Pete was sitting at the table with my friends, and Louise was standing behind him, smiling. But what made my heart leap was seeing Harry standing behind my empty chair, beaming at me. He hadn't left yet, after all.

I was so happy to see him that at first I didn't see who else was at the rest of the table. Bonnie looked at peace in a beautiful, soft, dove gray dress. Peggy reminded me of the celosia in my garden—red, yellow, and wearing something fluffy, her bracelets making rainbows whenever she moved her arm.

Faye wasn't in her seat. She was like a bee, moving from group to group and spreading joy everywhere. I could feel Harry behind me. Waiting. I was, too. There were three empty seats at the table, and I knew who they were for, but would they come?

And then I heard the voice I was longing for. "Happy birthday, mom," Jenny said. I looked up, and there she was. Grace was on one side of her, and Jack was on the other.

I thought at that moment I could never be happier, but later that day, my joy multiplied.

It happened at the end of the party. I was standing with Faye, Bonnie, and Peggy, thanking each person for coming. I heard Harry call me, and as I turned to his voice, time stopped, and for a minute I was in the future.

I was older, *still not looking too bad*, I thought, and then realized that was a ridiculous thing to be focusing on. Jenny and I were sitting at the tree table in my kitchen, and giggling together in the same way that we used to do when she was a little girl. She was describing what she and Jack were planning for a vacation. A gold ring on her finger told me they had married.

I heard Grace's footsteps as she came down the stairs and turned to see her carrying her new baby. I knew then that Grace and her husband would move in with me and have a son. His name would be Harry.

Time started up again. The future faded. But the present was just as wonderful, and I planned to stay in it as long as I could.

I made a silent promise that I was going to do my best to follow Peggy's advice and live out loud. I would make sure that every friend, every family member, would know how much I loved them.

At that moment, I knew I didn't need a book of memories to live my life. I would make memories instead. And then perhaps someday it would be Grace and her family who would find the memory book one morning and live these times again with me.

Author Note

I wanted to take my time writing this book. And I wanted to make it a stand-alone book that would shine by itself. Tell a story, once again, about women and friendship.

The story told itself. Little bits of this book are stories that came from my life or friends' lives, and I wove them into this story. I hope they brought the lives of Mabel, Peggy, Bonnie, Faye, and Grace to life for you.

Towards the end of the book, the plot twisted to include characters from the Ruby Sisters series. I hope you will be curious enough about Judith, Marshall, and Spring Falls to read the stories of five women who have been friends since elementary school as they uncover secrets and lies about their lives. I can promise you that, like in this book, everything will be well in the end.

Actually, all my fiction books contain references to each other. It's like one big universe, one that I hope you will enjoy entering and staying in for a while.

If you sign up for my mailing list, you'll be the first to know when new books arrive in this universe.

Most of all, thank you for being a reader of my books. It means the world to me.

249

Acknowledgements

I could never write a book without the help of my friends and my book community.

But as I mentioned in the dedication, my sister, always a beta reader, never got to read this book. On the other hand, it's possible that the ideas that came to me towards the end of writing this book came from her. So I send a thank you to you, Jamie, wherever you are.

But thankfully, I get to say thank you in person to Jet Tucker and Diana Cormier for taking the time to do the final reader proof. You can't imagine how much I appreciate it.

And as always, a huge thank you to Laura Moliter for her fantastic book editing.

Plus, thank you to every other member of my Book Community who helps me make so many decisions that help the book be the best book possible.

And a thank you to all the people who tell me they love to read these stories. Those random comments from friends and strangers are more valuable than gold.

And as always, thank you to my beloved husband, Del, for being my daily sounding board, for putting up with all my questions, my constant need to want to make things better, and for being the love of my life in more than just this one lifetime.

Also By Beca

Follow Me Here: **Women's Lit, Friendship**

The Rivers of Time Series: Women's Lit, Friendship

The Ruby Sisters Series: Women's Lit, Friendship
A Last Gift, After All This Time, And Then She Remembered, As If It Was Real, Almost Innocent

Stories From Doveland: Magical Realism, Friendship
Karass, Pragma, Jatismar, Exousia, Stemma, Paragnosis, In-Between, Missing, Out Of Nowhere

The Return To Erda Series: Fantasy
Shatterskin, Deadsweep, Abbadon, The Experiment

The Chronicles of Thamon: Fantasy
Banished, Betrayed, Discovered, Wren's Story

The Shift Series: Spiritual Self-Help
Living in Grace: The Shift to Spiritual Perception
The Daily Shift: Daily Lessons From Love To Money
The 4 Essential Questions: Choosing Spiritually Healthy Habits
The 28 Day Shift To Wealth: A Daily Prosperity Plan
The Intent Course: Say Yes To What Moves You
Imagination Mastery: A Workbook For Shifting Your Reality
Right Thinking: A Thoughtful System for Healing
Perception Mastery: Seven Steps To Lasting Change
Blooming Your Life: How To Experience Consistent Happiness

Perception Parables: Very short stories
Love's Silent Sweet Secret: A Fable About Love
Golden Chains And Silver Cords: A Fable About Letting Go

Advice:
A Woman's ABC's of Life: Lessons in Love, Life, and Career from
Those Who Learned The Hard Way
The Daily Nudge(s): So When Did You First Notice

About Beca

Beca writes books she hopes will change people's perceptions of themselves and the world, and open possibilities to things and ideas that are waiting to be seen and experienced.

At sixteen, Beca founded her own dance studio. Later, she received a Master's Degree in Dance in Choreography from UCLA and founded the Harbinger Dance Theatre, a multimedia dance company, while continuing to run her dance school.

After graduating—to better support her three children—Beca switched to the sales field, where she worked as an employee and independent contractor in many industries, excelling in each while perfecting and teaching her Shift System® and writing books.

She joined the financial industry in 1983, became an Associate Vice President of Investments at a major stock brokerage firm, and was a licensed Certified Financial Planner for over twenty years.

This diversity, along with a variety of life challenges, helped fuel the desire to share what she's learned by writing and speaking, hoping it will make a difference in other people's lives.

Beca grew up in State College, PA, with the dream of becoming a dancer and then a writer. She carried that dream forward as she fulfilled a childhood wish by moving to Southern California in 1968. Beca told her family she would never move back to the cold.

After living there for thirty-one years, she met her husband Delbert Lee Piper, Sr., at a retreat in Virginia, and everything changed. They decided to find a place they could call their own, which sent them off traveling around the United States. They lived and worked in a few different places before returning to live in the cold once again near Del's family in a small town in Northeast Ohio, not too far from State College.

When not working and teaching together, they love to visit and play with their combined family of eight children and five grandchildren, read, study, do yoga or taiji, feed birds, and work in their garden.